The Preacher's Legacy

Tom Deegan's fight for survival begins when he rescues a child from a burning stagecoach, held up by the murdering preacher and his gang. The preacher dies and Tom takes the loot and hides it.

Years later three killers are looking for Tom, and the money. But protecting himself, and his adopted son Billy, is only made more difficult by the local rancher, whose hired guns want Tom dead. By using his fighting skills can he protect them both? And can he remain silent about the whereabouts of the cash?

The Preacher's Legacy

Walter L. Bryant

A Black Horse Western

ROBERT HALE · LONDON

© Walter L. Bryant 2013
First published in Great Britain 2013

ISBN 978-0-7198-0872-2

Robert Hale Limited
Clerkenwell House
Clerkenwell Green
London EC1R 0HT

www.halebooks.com

Typeset by
Derek Doyle & Associates, Shaw Heath
Printed and bound in Great Britain by
CPI Antony Rowe, Chippenham and Eastbourne

PROLOGUE

As the shadows from horse and rider lengthened Tom Deegan sat his bay atop a rise and wished he was somewhere else. He took in a deep breath and held it as the stagecoach was dragged to a halt. Dust rose and hung in the air.

The four men on horseback held their guns steady. Through the bandanna that covered his mouth one of the men shouted, 'Throw yer weapons out an' step down from the coach.'

For the space of time it takes a rattlesnake to strike, there was silence. Nothing moved. Then, as if on a signal, the guard raised his shotgun and the driver's right hand snatched at his holster. At the same time a Colt sounded from within the coach.

Guns spat lead in a thunder of sound. The shotgun fired once before the man fell sideways and tumbled from his seat into the dirt. The driver, ducking down, fired over the top of the coach before he too was dead, blood already staining his clothes. Another member of the outlaw gang now directed his fire into the coach window.

Then suddenly, there was silence except for the snorting of the horses. Nobody moved.

Tom closed his eyes. As a lookout he had remained some way from the scene of death but was close enough to know that, even though he had not fired a shot, he shared the guilt with the others. The leader of the outlaw gang was his uncle, Morgan Jones, the respected preacher in the town of Salvation, who concealed his activities behind an aura of piety and respectability.

It was he who had insisted that Tom, at sixteen years of age, had to do his share. His share of what? Robbery and murder? Tom was sick of it. At least, in all the hold-ups he had witnessed so far, nobody had been killed. Now he had seen men being shot down needlessly and he wondered what would be found when the coach door was opened. He let his breath out in a long sigh.

Worse was to come. One of the outlaws had fallen from his horse and lay unmoving on the ground, his face blown away. When Tom looked again he saw that his uncle, the one who had issued the order, had sagged in the saddle and was holding his back where a bullet had entered.

One of the other men went over to support him while the third opened the coach door and peered inside. His shout caused the others to look up sharply.

'There's two men; one of 'em a guard, looks like, an' a dame,' he yelled. The others waited while he checked the bodies. When he emerged he called, 'All dead. An' we've shot a goddamn woman.'

Tom's uncle, recovering a little, moved across. 'Sure they're dead, Lofty?'

The coach door was slammed shut. 'Crow bait.'

'How the hell did this happen? Curly, get up on that coach an' throw down the cash so's we kin hightail it outa here.'

Tom was about to move forward when a rider came fast round the corner of the trail ahead. Without hesitation, Lofty raised his rifle and fired, the force of the shot lifting the rider from his saddle. The rider lay face up and it was clear he was young, about Tom's age, and had been of no obvious danger to the group other than maybe having ridden off to raise the alarm.

'Good shootin', Lofty', Tom's uncle growled. 'Now let's git going.'

The money, in a locked tin box, had been secured behind the driver. A bullet broke the lock and the contents were stuffed into saddle-bags.

The men rode to where Tom was waiting. 'You're gonna take the money,' his uncle said, grinding the words out through crippling pain. 'You're to stash it where we agreed and then go back to the house. Make out nothin's happened. We'll be there later to check the haul. Unnerstand? I gotta get this goddamn slug out.'

'What 'bout Jake?' Curly asked, pointing to the dead outlaw.

'He's past help,' Lofty said, grinning. 'Nothin' we kin do fer him. All the more fer us.'

Curly nodded and came up close to Tom. 'If we don't find the cash where it's supposed to be I'll come lookin' for ya,' he snarled into Tom's face. 'It's not too hard to figure out what'll happen then.'

Tom didn't argue. He was pleased to be leaving what had been an unnecessary massacre. He took the saddle-bags and waited as the gang rode away. He glanced down at the stagecoach where the team of horses was standing contentedly. When the coach failed to arrive at its destination, there would be men coming looking for it. But that would not be for a while yet.

Meantime the dead lay where they had fallen.

Tom waited motionless for some time – he had no idea how long – staring in shock and disgust at the carnage around the stage. Four bodies remained unmoving in the dirt and probably three more lay inside.

He shook himself out of his inaction, guided the bay closer, swung down and trailed the reins. His first duty, he had decided, was to check the bodies for any signs of life, which the outlaws had failed to do. He took a deep breath and began his gruesome inspection.

The young boy he took first. He ran swiftly over to him but there was no hope there; a slug had taken him full in the chest and he lay in a pool of blood. The driver and the guard had also received fatal shots to the heart, head and other parts of their bodies. There was nothing he could do for any of them.

While he was carrying out this unwelcome task he failed to notice the restlessness of the horses, not only those harnessed to the stagecoach but also his own. When he became aware of their behaviour he looked about, expecting to see something or someone that was spooking them.

Then he smelled it; smoke issuing through the windows of the vehicle. And he heard it, too, the faint but ominous crackle of flames as they took hold of the wood and materials within.

Assuming that the three in the coach were dead, his first thoughts were for the team of horses, already showing alarm, snorting and bucking in the shafts. He had to unhitch them, not an easy task with the animals quickly becoming out of control and likely to take off with the burning coach trailing behind them.

It took him precious minutes, by which time his arms were cut and bruised as they were trapped between the horses' flanks and the shafts. The frightened animals needed no encouragement and raced away as soon as they were free.

By this time flames were leaping from the coach window. He had to get the bodies out so at least somebody might recognize them. He couldn't leave them to burn. He raced to open the coach door and the flames met him, searing his skin, hair and clothes with their intense heat.

He was surprised how swiftly the fire was taking hold. The occupants had not moved. One man, dressed in black, was still holding a Colt in his right hand and, bizarrely, a cigar in the other. Even through the flames Tom could see the blood staining their clothes. The woman's cotton dress was burning and the man's heavier jacket and pants smouldering. He held his breath and reached in, grabbed the woman's arm and pulled. Her body slipped to the floor.

As her head fell from the seat Tom froze.

A small child, probably not yet one year old, lay in the corner. Apparently the child's mother had protected it from stray bullets while she had been alive and now her body had become a shield against the fire.

Tom's eyes rounded, then he gritted his teeth in anger that his uncle could so callously abandon a child to its fate. He didn't hesitate. With the flames now licking up to the roof he reached in, grabbed the child and pulled it clear, feeling his own flesh scorching as he did so. Holding the small body awkwardly, he backed away from the inferno and laid the child well clear of the blazing coach.

He went back but knew he could do no more. He staggered away, sank to the ground next to the child and watched as the last remnants of the vehicle collapsed. Now the danger had passed, his own legs felt weak and his injuries were causing him pain.

'Well,' he muttered when he'd recovered from his exertions, 'what am I goin' to do with you?' He had little experience of young children.

The child's big, frightened eyes looked up at him, mouth open, but no sound came out.

'No cause to be scared of me,' Tom said and broke into a cautious smile as he considered the situation that now confronted him: saddle-bags full of money, a young child to take care of and burns to his face and hands.

He was aware, also, that the fire, the smoke and the runaway team of horses would soon bring someone to the scene.

10

His own horse had wandered off to where it was contentedly eating grass. When he felt strong enough he wrapped the child in its shawl, carried him across, spoke softly to the animal and remounted with the trembling child carefully held to his body.

He had now started to think more clearly. When a posse arrived, as they surely would, they would read his tracks on the ground and would know there had been a fifth member of the gang. If they were good at their job they would then track him.

Reason told him he had to follow the course that the other outlaws had taken even though this took him away from town. At the first opportunity, when the ground was hard and left no prints, he could turn away and eventually double back. But then what?

He knew what he had to do. The only safe place he could take the child was to his aunt's, the sister of the preacher. She would know what to do.

To hell with the money. He'd decide about that later.

He rode carefully without looking back, the scene imprinted on his mind. How could such a thing have happened? If he hadn't been there the small child would have been killed. As it was, the fire had destroyed everything that could have told him the child's identity.

At first he carried the child, cradled in one arm, then, as this became tiring, over his shoulder. Finally, from his Stetson, his vest and his neckerchief he fashioned a passable seat soft enough for the child to sit on, holding on to the small body with one hand and taking the reins in the other. All the while the child was silent and uncomplaining, making the journey much easier

11

than it might otherwise have been.

On the edge of the town of Salvation a small group of houses stood, separated from the town itself by a stand of trees. Between them and the town the white-painted church was a monument to what the townsfolk considered to be their preacher's purity of thought and deed. The bell tower, large and ornate, had been built to the design of the preacher, who had also provided the money to pay for it.

Tom reined in at the end house, set neatly in a garden bordered by a white-painted fence and hedgerows. He dismounted and looked around, trusting that his aunt would be in at this time of day. Aunt Jane was his only hope.

He was relieved to hear some activity in the back yard and when he called out, his aunt appeared round the corner of the building. Jane Cosby was a small woman of forty, round-faced with prematurely greying hair pulled into a bun behind her head. Her smile was always ready for her friends and family.

She peered at the bundle in Tom's arms. 'What. . . ?' she began but drew in her breath when she saw what Tom was carrying. 'Who. . . ?' She pushed the shawl aside and looked down into the terrified eyes of the small child. 'How did you. . . ?'

'I need to come in,' Tom said. 'There's something I've gotta tell you. Need ya help.'

His aunt didn't hesitate, her motherly instincts responding immediately to the emergency. She led the way into the small front room, indicating that they should both sit down before launching into explanations. 'Well?' she said.

Tom, still holding the child, talked quickly, telling his aunt of the hold-up, the killings, the fire, but leaving out the fact that outside were saddle-bags full of stolen money.

'Uncle's bin wounded,' he said. 'Dunno how bad.'

'I wouldn't turn a hair if he was burned in hell,' Aunt Jane said with unaccustomed venom. 'Anyone who can preach the word of God and do the things he did deserves to die.' She crossed herself. 'And you're telling me you had no part in this?'

'I saw it happen,' Tom said. 'There wasn't nothing I could do. 'Cept save this little boy. Or girl,' he added.

'We'll soon see which,' Aunt Jane said, and then reached across and took the bundle from his arms. 'Oh! But you're hurt.' She peered at the burns on Tom's hands and arms. 'We'll have to get those treated.'

She lay the child down, making sure it was comfortable, then turned her attention to Tom. She fetched ointment and bandages, dressed his wounds and snipped off the burnt portions of his hair. 'That'll do until you can see the doc,' she said, then she turned her attention to examining the child. 'It's a boy and he seems unhurt, thanks to you. Now, the question is, what are we going to do with him?'

'I was sorta hoping you might—'

'Definitely not!'

'We can't let him go into an orphanage,' Tom said. 'Uncle Morgan, for all his faults, kept me outa that sorta place. You could look after him fer a time an' then I could take over in a coupla years.'

'You don't know what you're asking. The boy's got family somewhere. They'll have to be found, if possible.'

Tom was quiet for several minutes as he chewed on his lips. 'OK. But if nobody turns up will you do it?'

Jane studied her nephew's face and reached a decision. 'I could do it but not for long. I've a business to run. I'll need help, of course, but that can be arranged with not too many questions being asked.'

'Thanks, Aunt Jane! I don't know how—'

'But folk will have to know where he was found. They don't need to know how you were involved. You saw the fire and rescued him. That's all we say. Can you manage that?'

Tom nodded enthusiastically.

'And,' his aunt went on, 'if nobody claims him we'll have to get a court order giving you custody of the boy when you're old enough.'

Tom put his arms around his aunt and hugged her tight.

All he had to do now was hide a sizeable bundle of money and no one, not even his aunt, was going to know about that. If she'd thought to ask, though, he doubted he could have lied to her.

CHAPTER 1

Tom Deegan, now twenty-nine years old and over six feet tall, was powerful, slim of hip, broad of shoulder and self-assured, yet still had bad dreams of the time, thirteen years ago, when he watched the killing of six people in cold blood. Billy, the boy he had carried in his arms that day and had since taken on as his own son, was a continual reminder. As if he needed one.

He watched now as Billy toiled in the hot sun, wielding a heavy axe as he built up a pile of logs for the winter. Tom was proud of him. At nearly fourteen, Billy was determined to do a man's work.

Tom feared sometimes that he asked too much of the boy, although he knew that at a similar age he had grafted from sunup to sundown on his uncle's farm, and even then his day's work was far from finished.

But then, he had done it from fear and because he'd be beaten if he failed. Billy did it because he wanted to. Tom recalled those days with some bitterness but also with satisfaction and pride that the hard work his uncle had forced upon him had toughened him, made him self-sufficient, determined to make him craft his own future.

He was also grateful to his uncle for taking him in when it was likely he would have ended up in an orphanage, although he had been aware for some time that he had been expected to become a full gang member as soon as he was old enough.

When he was sixteen that phase of his life had ended after his uncle died from a bullet in the spine. That had been the outcome of the outlaw band's last fatal hold-up and Tom had not grieved for a second. During the following years he had grown in strength and height until now, with steel-grey eyes and a firm set to his mouth, he was the match of any man.

'Finish up now, Billy,' he called. 'I'm goin' up to the meadow. Back in an hour. Expect some chow ready by then. An' I'd 'preciate it if it was edible this time.'

'OK, Pa.' Billy glanced up. 'I cook better'n you any day.'

Tom smiled and knew without looking that his son would follow his progress all the way up the slope until he disappeared over the rise. He waved but didn't look back.

The two horsemen rode into the yard and up to the front door of the cabin where Billy was standing, watching out for the return of his pa. The stew was in the pot and the coffee strong and hot as his pa liked it.

The men remained in their saddles as their eyes swept around. Billy didn't like the look of them, knew they were trouble before they spoke. Both were dressed in black and had the appearance of being something other than mere cowhands.

'Where's yer pa, son?'

Billy didn't like being called son. 'Who wants to know?'

'I asked you a question, son. Is he around or not?' The man who spoke, lean and swarthy, slid from the saddle and advanced a few steps. As he came closer Billy noticed the Colt, low-slung, tied down at his hip.

'I didn't say you could git off'n yer horse,' Billy said, trying to keep the tremble from his voice. 'Whatever you have to say you kin say to me.'

The man narrowed his eyes. 'We wanna talk to yer pa. Go git him.'

Billy was not about to do anything that would mean leaving the cabin unguarded. Trouble was, he'd be powerless to prevent the men from entering the property if they took it into their heads to do so. For one thing, he wasn't wearing a gun and, even if he had been, he couldn't take on these two gunslingers if they had a mind to draw on him.

'He's busy. Guess you'd better come back tomorrow.' His pa had told him that if the odds were against you, bluff it out; never show fear. That's just what he was trying to do and he wasn't certain it was working.

The men appeared undecided. 'Don't appreciate yer attitude, son.' The second man spoke for the first time. 'But you kin give yer pa a message.' He glanced across at his pard. 'Tell him we've come to warn him.'

'Warn him about what?'

'Seems like the farmers and sodbusters round here

need to be protected an' we're jus' the men to do it.'

'Who's doin' the attacking?' It was the first Billy had heard of it and he was sure his pa would've mentioned something like that.

'Don't matter who.' A note of annoyance had crept into the man's tone. 'Jus' tell yer pa what we said.' His hard eyes fixed on Billy. 'Him with a young boy like you to look after could do with some protection.'

Now it was Billy's turn to get angry. 'I don't need lookin' after. I kin take care of myself. So kin Pa.'

'That so? Just give him the message.'

Billy was about to make some retort when he caught sight of his pa returning. His eyes must have given him away, for both men turned.

'Guess ya kin give it to him yerself,' Billy said as Tom reined in behind the men. He looked at his son for an explanation.

'They come to warn ya,' Billy said.

Tom turned his attention to the men and his face hardened. 'Obliged,' he said.

'There's bin trouble hereabouts.'

'Yeah?'

'Yep.'

'An' just who am I indebted to fer this information?'

'Name's Dutch. This here's Carlos.'

'Well, Dutch an' Carlos, don't reckon I know yer.'

'Work at the Triple O,' Dutch said.

'An' what kinda work might that be?' Tom asked, eyeing their weaponry.

Dutch ignored the question. 'We kin help ya protect yersel's seein' as ya short-handed here an' got a boy an' all.' He leered at Billy.

'Mighty civil of ya.'

'But it'll cost,' Carlos grinned.

'How much?'

'Hundred'll do as a start.'

'Well, that's a generous offer,' Tom drawled. 'Tell ya what. I'll give ya a hundred seconds to git off my land or it'll be you needin' protection.' Without warning a gun appeared in his hand. 'Git back in yer saddle. I don't wanna see you round here agin.'

Billy couldn't help smiling at the scowls that appeared on the men's faces. For a second he expected them to draw their own weapons but the moment passed. Without another word they wheeled their horses and rode out. One turned and yelled, 'You'll regret this.'

Tom didn't bother to reply.

'Gunnies, pure an' simple,' he told Billy. 'From the Triple O. Looking fer a cheap buck or, more likely, to scare us off.' He laid his hand on Billy's head. 'You did well. You've been a great help to me these past few years. Between us we've built a real good place here.'

'I know that, Pa.' Billy grinned. 'You couldn't've done it without me.'

'Can't disagree with that. You've done enough fer today, son. Time fer grub.'

Although he had outwardly dismissed the incident it had helped Tom in his decision to take Billy to a place of safety. The biggest threat now was not the two men he had just seen off his property but the release from prison of Curly Thomson and Lofty Tate, the outlaws from his uncle's gang.

Knowing the day would come when they had completed their sentence, he had kept track, through newspapers and other means, of the time they had served. It had come as a shock when he learned they had been paroled after only thirteen years. He knew they would come looking and they would find him sooner or later. He had to be ready.

He deeply regretted having to send Billy away for a while but it was for his own safety and would give him more freedom to act. He'd made up his mind; he would do it the following day. He waited until the day's work was almost over.

'Supper time, Billy,' he called.

'I'm OK,' Billy said. 'There's another half hour o' the day left an' I need to get some feed fer the horses.'

The boy was tall for his age but his body was rapidly filling out and his arms were strong. His fair hair blew about his neck and face.

Tom left his son to finish off while he washed under the pump, revelling in the feel of the cold water over his back and face. He felt good. He was fit, strong. The days when he had lived with the preacher after his parents died were now just a bad memory.

He replaced his shirt and took a moment to pass his gaze over his property. Small though it was, he owned it outright and he was proud of the way in which he had developed it. He owed nothing to anybody and could more than pay his way.

To his surprise the preacher had made a will leaving the small farm to him and he had no conscience at using what money there had been, reasoning that he had never seen a cent from the sale of his own parents' assets. As for his Aunt Jane, she would have nothing to do with anything her brother had owned.

After eating, Tom and Billy remained seated, Tom savouring his coffee and Billy pretending to enjoy it.

'I'm gonna take ya to stay with yer Aunt Jane fer a while,' Tom said, breaking the silence.

Billy looked up quickly, his face showing his disbelief. 'But, Pa.' He thought for a moment. 'Why're you doing that? How'm I gonna do the chores if I'm not here? How'll you manage?'

'It's for ya own good, son,' Tom said. 'It'll only be fer a few days but I need to know you're safe.'

'Won't you be safe?'

'It could get a mite dangerous round here afore long an' I need you outa the way. There's two men'll wanna discuss some business with me.'

'But, Pa.'

'Sorry, son. No argument. We'll set off at sunup. Best pack a few things.' There was no more discussion and Billy spoke little for the rest of the evening. Tom wished he could explain more but now was not the time. After an early breakfast the following morning, they set off.

Much as it pained him Tom knew he was doing the right thing. With Curly Thomson and Lofty Tate loose there was likely to be lead flying. He had to be ready.

They had been travelling for twenty minutes – Billy still resentful, his pa sympathetic but adamant – when Tom reined the grey in silently and signalled to Billy to do the same.

He was immediately alert as he topped the rise. His mount had given warning before he became aware of the small group of men and horses gathered under a stand of trees where the trail dipped and curved round.

He screwed up his eyes against the glare of the morning sun and assessed the scene below. As he watched, a man with his hands secured behind his back was brought forward and hoisted onto a buckskin horse. It was then he saw the rope that had been slung over a sturdy branch.

Tom tightened his jaw and turned to the boy who had reined in beside him. 'Keep outa sight, Billy, I'm goin' in closer.' He wheeled the grey and set off down a gully, which would provide concealment. He loosened the Winchester in its scabbard.

'I'm comin' with you,' Billy said and followed, crouching low over the bay's neck in the same way as his pa was doing.

The gully petered out and the two slid from their saddles. Now it was clear what was about to happen. A noose had already been slipped over the man's head as he sat astride the horse. Two men stood silently by.

'What we gonna do, Pa?' the boy asked.

'You ain't doin nothin' Billy. Nor'm I.' He had quickly assessed the situation. On his own he might have called a warning to stop the men from carrying out the lynching. But he couldn't risk a gunfight with the boy by his side. 'We'll wait.'

The waiting didn't take long.

Tom saw there was a discussion going on between two of the men that he was unable to hear, but the laughter indicated that they considered the situation funny. The third man with the rope around his neck clearly did not see the joke. It occurred to Tom that a mock trial was taking place, the prisoner trying to argue his case, but hampered by the ropes binding him.

The trial was over quickly, the verdict predictable.

At a silent signal the buckskin was given a hard slap on the rump, leaving the victim swinging on the end of the rope. Without a word the men wheeled their mounts and rode away at full gallop, trailing the buckskin with them.

Tom allowed them to cover some distance before he withdrew the Bowie knife from its sheath and urged the grey forward. One sweep of the sharp blade severed the rope and, even before the man had fallen, Tom had leaped from the saddle.

'Is he alive, Pa?' Billy breathed.

Tom loosened the noose and listened to the rasp of the man's breath as he forced air into his lungs. 'They beat him up some afore they hanged him, but he'll live,' he said as he noticed the bruising about the man's face.

He let some water from his canteen trickle down the man's throat. 'Take it easy,' he said. He sat him up and leaned him against the tree, then turned to his son. 'We'd best get away from here. Those *hombres* might just decide to come back an' check on their handiwork.'

He lifted the man to his feet and helped him walk the short distance into the cover of the trees. 'Should be OK here.' He glanced up at the man he had rescued, noticing for the first time the look of anxiety in his eyes. 'What's yer name?'

He was certainly no hard man, dressed as he was in broadcloth coat and black boots. He was, Tom judged, about fifty years old with a weather-beaten face and hands more suited to the soil than the gun. His eyes, a startling blue, were alert despite the ordeal he had just gone through.

'You gotta name?' Tom asked.

'Dave Green.' He took another sip of water. 'I'm obliged to you. An' the boy. Reckon I'd be meetin' my Maker if you two hadn't bin around.'

'Why'd they string you up?'

'Rustlin'. They figured I'd bin stealin' their cattle.'

'An' were you stealin' cattle?'

'Nope. An' they knew darned well I wasn't but that didn't bother 'em none.' He levered himself to his feet and a look of panic suddenly flared in his eyes. 'I gotta get back home. They were talkin' 'bout my wife. That's where they'll be makin' fer.'

'You've no horse an' no gun,' Tom pointed out. 'You can't do much on yer own.'

Dave Green looked longingly at Billy's horse, then let his gaze fall on the carbine nestling in its scabbard.

Tom smiled grimly. 'You may have a chance if we come with you but I don't want to put the boy in any danger. You OK with that?'

He gestured to his son. 'You ride up with me.'

He withdrew his Winchester and handed it to the other man but before letting go of it he said, 'There's another condition. We do this my way or not at all. We

24

stay together. OK?' He reached down and pulled his son up in front. 'Let's go.'

CHAPTER 2

'Yer leaving us, then?' the prison guard asked with a grin that seemed to say, 'I'll still be here when ya return.'

Curly Thomson and Lofty Tate grinned back. If they had any say in the matter they would never be returning.

'Yeah,' Curly drawled. 'We got important matters to attend to.'

'Thought ya liked it here.'

'What gave ya that idea?'

The guard, seemingly annoyed that he no longer had control of these two prisoners, rapped his club against his palm. 'It's bin a real pleasure gettin' you two in line. I'll look forward to seein' you again.'

'Oh, you might at that,' Lofty said. 'But this time we'll be on the outside. And,' he added, with a barely concealed threat, 'we'll be lookin' out for ya.'

'Oh, I'm scared, real scared,' the guard yawned dramatically.

As the two men left the prison for the last time they intended never to set eyes on it again for the rest of their lives. The thirteen years during which they had been incarcerated behind its forbidding walls had seemed to stretch forever.

They were so intent on getting away that they failed to see the shadowy figure who trailed them almost as soon as they left the gates. Even had they looked they would have seen nothing because the man who followed them was an expert in his chosen profession.

'What're ya gonna do with yer share?' Lofty asked.

'Dunno yet,' Curly said. 'From what I saw in that tin box I'll be able to buy anythin' I want.'

'Half-share's mine,' Lofty said quickly.

Curly realized his mistake. He had no intention of sharing with anyone. 'Yeah, that's what I meant. We should stick together.'

In fact Curly had been the dominant partner while they had been imprisoned and Lofty knew it. He had realized early on that to survive he had to put his trust in Curly. Lately he had begun not to trust him at all.

The years inside had changed them, as had the hard labour they had endured, the vicious guards and the poor food. At the beginning of their sentence, before their muscles had hardened and before they had earned some respite for good behaviour, they had found the work almost too much. Punishments were frequent and severe, testing their spirit and their mutual pact to keep silent about the loot from their last robbery.

As time progressed their bodies and their minds became accustomed to the routine. They settled, looking out for each other when the occasion demanded, determined to earn a remission of their sentence. Their resolve had remained as strong as ever.

At their trial they had tried to argue that, although they had fired some shots in self-defence, it had been the preacher and Jake who'd been responsible for the killings. The judge had not been inclined to believe them but he had been lenient, sentencing them to twenty years. They should have had more, but the judge, wishing to prove his credentials as a man of God and being angry at the preacher for betraying his calling, was more lenient with them than they deserved.

'I reckon you should never have killed him,' Curly said suddenly, a note of censure in his voice.

'Who ya talkin' about?'

'The preacher.'

'Don't see why not. He was dyin' anyway. Holdin' us up.'

'He should've tasted prison, same as us.'

Lofty shook his head violently. 'Naw. Better off where he is.'

'Mebbe if he'd bin alive we'd never have got caught.'

Lofty sneered. 'With him bein' dead we could put the blame on him fer hidin' the cash an' leadin' us astray.'

Curly had to laugh at that.

Now free, they looked forward to reaping their reward. The thought of that had kept them going as other men had given up or died from the tough prison regime. They were still young enough to enjoy the rest of their lives in luxury. This thought had driven them on. They were changed men, though not for the better.

Their hair and the stubble on their chins was longer,

their tempers shorter, their moustaches more luxuri-
ant. And whereas before they had been content to allow
their bodies to put on excess weight, they were now
much leaner with muscles as hard as the rocks they had
been forced to quarry.

The work had been tough, exhausting, but they had
learned how to survive. They *had* survived.

With the few dollars they had with them, some of
which had been provided by kindly women of the local
temperance charity, which gave funds to help reformed
criminals, they were ready to equip themselves with
mounts and guns.

The ladies had said, 'You promise, gentlemen, that
you'll forswear the demon drink and the temptations of
the flesh from this day?' and they had readily given
their word.

Their first thoughts after accepting the money continued to be for liquor and women. Once those desires
had been satisfied, they could think about recovering
the money.

Slim Newman lay belly-down on a rocky escarpment, his
long, slender body spread eagled comfortably as he sur-
veyed the two men below him. He was curious as he
watched them pulling loose rocks away from a boulder
at the edge of an outcrop within easy rifle range from
where he waited.

He had decided he would allow Curly and Lofty their
brief moment of satisfaction and triumph before he
shot them dead.

His face was set in hard lines, his lips thin, a short,

downward-sloping moustache doing nothing to soften the sharp lines of cruelty etched there. He was dressed in brown with a grey Stetson pushed back to cover his neck.

His horse, a chestnut, was ground-tethered behind him and out of sight. His rifle, a Winchester .38-.40, rested by his side, ready for use.

He was sweating from the heat. The rocks on which he lay were hot to the touch, having baked in the sun for much of the day. He cursed at the discomfort but knew he would not have long to wait.

Slim had been a very successful bounty hunter but he was past his prime and the years were catching up with him. The dangerous nature of his profession had taken its toll. Although his reflexes were still unimpaired, his draw as lightning fast as ever, his eyes were not as keen as they once were.

The time had come to quit, to find a new and less hazardous profession, but one that would pay as well. And he had found it.

The two men toiling on the plain below had committed robbery and murder and because of that, if for no other reason, he considered that he was as much entitled to the proceeds of their last venture as they were.

With the experience of many years' hunting men he had positioned himself with the sun behind him and had dulled the barrel of his gun. There was no need to advertise his presence now the time had come to end the chase after nearly three days on the trail. He knew what the men were looking for and he was content to let them find it.

He had patiently waited while they had satisfied their needs. Now they had led him here. Although they didn't know it, this would be the end of their journey. He watched as the boulder rolled away, disclosing an opening large enough for a man to enter. A moment later there was an anguished cry.

'There's nothin'! It's gone!'

The second man checked and his search came up with the same result.

The conversation that followed was inaudible but it was clear that the discovery had caused confusion.

Slim let out a sigh. He remained perfectly still.

Just as well he had held his fire; the game wasn't over yet.

The men's consternation at discovering that the money had not been stashed as agreed had quickly turned to anger. They mounted their horses, both of which had seen better days, and set off to track down the man responsible for stealing what was rightfully theirs: Tom Deegan.

If they didn't find him at his home, they would follow him no matter where.

'That young varmint's gonna be feeding the coyotes when I git my hands on him,' Curly growled.

'Not afore he's told us what we wanna know,' Lofty said.

A wicked smile split Curly's face. 'I hope he needs jus' a little persuading.'

'Even if he don't . . .' Lofty left the sentence unfinished but a light glowed in his eyes.

The money was theirs. They had worked for it. They'd spent thirteen years of their lives dreaming about it.

It was in this mood that they approached Hope Springs, a small developing town some twelve miles from Salvation, their ultimate destination. Keen as they were to get there they did not want to arrive at night.

Of the competing desires of money, liquor and women, the first was what drove them on. Nevertheless, given that the last two were immediately available in Hope Springs, Curly and Lofty made straight for the only saloon that the town appeared to possess. Only later did they realize how hungry they were.

The town consisted of a short main street on both sides of which signs of extensive new building work was evident. There were stores and shops where basic materials could be obtained, a livery, a law office, which was no more than a wooden hut, a hotel and an eating house, the Roll-up café.

A sign on the door of the eating house informed them that the place was closing for the night.

'My belly's flapping agin my spine,' Lofty complained as he put his shoulder to the door. It opened easily enough and the pleasing aroma of coffee and freshly baked bread hung in the air. Inside, three tables, covered in white linen cloths, were occupied where diners were finishing their meals.

A woman, well past the bloom of youth, dressed in a floral cotton dress covered by a clean white apron, came up to them with a friendly smile of apology. She had a thin face with tired grey eyes and, although few would call her beautiful, she may well have been good-looking some years back.

'Sorry, gents; serving's finished for the day.'

Lofty pointed to the diners. 'They're eatin' and we're hungry as bears.' He pulled out a chair and sat at a table against the wall. 'Steak with plenty of gravy,' he said. 'And be quick about it.'

Curly joined him and grinned up at the woman. 'Best do what he says. Don't want no trouble.' His eyes told a different story.

The woman seemed as though she would argue but thought better of it, looked for support from the other folk present and found none. She frowned, turned on her heel and went back to the kitchen.

As the men waited Curly's gaze swept round the room. At one table a young man and woman, probably still in their twenties, were gazing into each other's eyes, ignoring the food in front of them. The girl was pretty with an oval face framed by long flaxen hair. Her hand held that of her companion under the table.

At another table two men in overalls were finishing off the last remnants of some apple pie.

The occupant of the third table held Curly's attention for a while longer. From the way he sat with his long legs stretched out it was clear to Curly that the man was tall and slim. When he glanced up his eyes were cold. There was something dangerous about him that demanded caution.

Curly and Lofty ate ravenously when the meal came, Lofty calling for a second helping.

'I'm sorry,' the woman said, brushing the hair back

from her forehead. 'There's no more till tomorrow.'

Lofty shot out his hand and grabbed the woman by the arm, pulling her closer until she could smell the whiskey on his breath. 'If there ain't no more grub, I'll make do with you, you little whore,' he grated and roared with laughter at his own wit.

'Leave me alone!' She struggled against Lofty's superior strength as she felt her mouth being drawn down towards his.

A scraping of chairs alerted Curly, who leaped to his feet, drawing his gun at the same time. 'Anybody wants to play is OK by me,' he said coldly.

The two workmen left hurriedly. The two lovers hesitated too long. The slim man had not moved.

The woman continued to fight, turned her face away and pushed against Lofty hard so that he lost his balance on the chair and toppled over backwards. As he fell he released his grip and the woman took advantage, scurrying away, back to the kitchen.

'You ugly bitch,' Lofty shouted after her. 'Who the hell'd want ya, anyway?' He picked himself up while he searched the room for anyone who might consider the situation funny. His eyes met those of Slim and he quickly turned away, his gaze settling on the girl who, with her escort, had risen and was preparing to leave.

'C'mere,' Lofty grated. 'No call to leave so soon.'

The young couple said nothing as they hastened to the exit, only to find that Lofty had beaten them to it and stood barring their progress. 'Young an' pretty, jus' as I like 'em.' Lofty licked his lips and grasped a handful of the girl's hair.

She tried to pull away as the young man came between them. 'Let her go!' he shouted, but any further action he might have been contemplating was cut short as Curly brought the barrel of his gun to the side of his head. He sank to the floor.

Slim watched with an amused smile and was still seated when the marshal arrived. The lawman was big but overweight so that his six-gun was almost hidden by his belly. 'What's bin goin' on?' he demanded breathlessly.

'A little horseplay,' Curly said. 'Nothin' more.'

The marshal looked at the girl as she helped the young man to his feet. 'Is that right, Nancy?'

She opened her mouth to say something, then thought better of it as she felt Curly's eyes upon her. At last she said, 'Yes, that's all it was, Marshal.'

The law officer turned his gaze on Curly and Lofty. 'How long yer meaning to stay in Hope Springs?'

'Leavin' at sunup, Marshal,' Curly said. 'This seems like an unfriendly sorta place.'

'Headin' fer where?'

'Salvation, Marshal.'

Slim, listening to this, smiled to himself as if that was just the information he needed.

The marshal gestured towards the door. 'OK, you two git out of here. I don't reckon to see you tomorrow but if you cause any more trouble in my town you'll be spendin' the rest of yer stay behind bars.'

After watching them leave he glanced over at Slim. 'Is that all it was? Horseplay?'

'Somethin' like that,' Slim told him.

35

'Why in hell didn't ya do somethin' to stop it?' His eyes glanced down at the gun nestling on Slim's hip.

Slim raised his eyebrows, indicating that the answer was obvious. 'The man had a gun, Marshal.'

The marshal drew a deep breath of frustration. 'The same warning as I gave them other two goes fer you.'

'I'll bear that in mind, Marshal,' Slim said softly.

Before eating, Slim had booked the last available room at the hotel so Curly and Lofty were forced to spend the night in the hayloft at the livery. This did not improve their tempers and it was with ill-humour the following day that they approached Salvation.

Their first impression was that it was larger than when they had left. More buildings lined the main street and it seemed that there was a greater number of people and horses. New stores had opened. Even a new saloon had sprung up.

They marked that for an immediate visit. Maybe there were possibilities for winning a few dollars at the tables so they could buy themselves better horses.

Both men had changed to such an extent that nobody seemed to recognize them. This suited them well. They wondered if Buck Clements still occupied the law office in Salvation and whether he would recall who they were. More importantly, if he would be able to give them news of the man they sought. Perhaps an early call on him would bring results.

As they stood outside the office both men noticed the stranger who dismounted in front of the newspaper office ten minutes after they had entered the town. It would have been difficult to miss him, a striking figure, tall and slim, riding a handsome chestnut.

Curly opened his mouth to say something, then changed his mind.

CHAPTER 3

Tom, with Billy holding on in front of him, set off at a good speed, glancing behind at Dave Green, who was keeping pace. He eased the grey after ten minutes. As they rode the farmer explained that he had had several visits from the group of men and every time they had demanded payment in return for protection.

'Protection against what?' Tom asked.

'Bandits, apparently,' Dave said. 'An' outlaws. I ain't never seen any. Guess they must've bin talkin' about theirselves.'

'Yeah, I had a visit from two of 'em yesterday,' Tom said.

Dave had refused to pay and at each visit the demands had grown more aggressive. This last time the men had decided to make an example of him and his family.

'They tied up my wife and daughter and, after hanging me fer rustlin', they were going back to the house. I pray we're not too late.'

'No point in killing the horses,' Tom said, seeing that

the farmer was eager to push on, 'or we won't get there at all. How much further?'

Dave pointed. 'Jest over that hill an' we ride down into the valley. We settled by the bend in the river.'

'Any way of getting to the house without being seen?' Dave shook his head.

'None at all. It's all open ground.'

'OK, so we move in quietly from the rear. If they're there they won't be expecting trouble.' He spoke to Billy. 'Soon as we crest the rise you're gonna get off and stay hidden.'

'But, Pa, I kin handle a gun. You taught me.'

'I also taught ya when to avoid trouble,' Tom said. 'An' this is one of those times.'

From the top of the rise Tom saw the house nestling below. It looked peaceful enough with a thin wisp of smoke rising from the chimney, a milk cow in the back field, chickens in the yard, two horses in the small corral and three horses out front. He knew appearances were deceptive because he recognized the buckskin he had last seen at the lynching.

They approached quietly towards the back of the building where there was only one window. Tom held up his hand and indicated that they should dismount. He did not want the nickering of a horse giving warning of their presence.

He had already outlined his plan to Dave and thirty feet from the rear wall, they parted. Dave angled to the side while Tom went around and then walked openly to the front door.

He pushed back his Stetson, knocked and stepped

back a few paces. With no response he knocked louder and waited. A voice, perhaps trying and failing to sound friendly, called through the wooden panel of the door. 'Who is it? What d'ya want?'

'Rest an' water fer me and my horse if you kin oblige,' Tom replied. 'I've bin travellin' far.'

The door opened. The man who stood there with his hand resting on his holster was short but broad-shouldered, dressed smartly in black jeans and shirt. His face held a scowl as if he'd been disturbed. His gaze searched for Tom's horse and suspicion crept into his eyes. 'Who are ya? I reckon I've seen ya before.' Recognition flared. 'Yeah, I should've knowed. Yer the varmint who said he didn't want our protection.'

'Yep, I know you, too, ya sonofabitch,' Tom snarled. 'An' I still don't want protection. Mebbe it's you that needs it.'

The man showed his teeth in a snarl and snatched his gun from its holster. Tom couldn't risk waiting. 'Now!' he roared and his own gun leaped into his hand. Almost as fast but not quick enough, the man raised his pistol and Tom was left with no choice.

The thunder of his Colt mingled with the sound of breaking glass and the roar of a Winchester as Dave opened fire through the window.

As the noise died away Tom stepped over the dead body and made his way cautiously into the house. From a room on his left he heard the excited cries of two women and the comforting voice of Dave as he clambered through the shattered window.

A man lay dead on the floor while the two women,

who had been securely bound to their chairs, were quite clearly in shock.

'Nice shootin',' Tom said, releasing the girl while Dave saw to his wife.

'Thank God you're safe,' Dave breathed as he embraced them both.

His wife, tears coursing down her cheeks, said, 'I thought you were dead.'

'Would've bin,' Dave said, 'but fer this gentleman. We owe him more than we kin ever repay.'

While Tom was busy denying that they were in any way indebted to him his eyes were fixed on the girl. He guessed she would be about twenty-three. She was a beautiful young woman in every sense with long flaxen hair, an oval face and eyes of the purest blue. Her simple white blouse was ripped at the front.

'I'll be back in a moment,' he mumbled in some confusion and went outside to signal for Billy.

When he returned he was introduced to Tom's wife, Mary, and his daughter, Alice, who had now changed her clothes and, in spite of her frightening ordeal, appeared self-possessed and able to smile. And that smile won Tom over completely.

Dave took the bodies outside while Tom and Billy were urged to sit down at the family table and accept the hospitality of the home.

As they ate soup and drank homemade cordial Dave became more and more restless. 'They ain't gonna get away with this,' he growled.

'Who are they?' Tom asked.

'John Gordon and his bunch of hard cases,' Dave said.

41

Tom had been aware of the activities of the local rancher and knew that some of the things he had done were at the edge of the law, but he found it hard to believe that he was behind the behaviour he had witnessed. He expressed these views to Dave.

The farmer shook his head. 'You may be right but I'm sure as hell gonna find out. Sorry, Mary,' he said when she raised her eyebrows at his language.

'Just let it go,' his wife urged. 'There's no good will come of all this.'

'I'm gonna show John Gordon that he can't push people around jest to suit hisself.' Dave stood up. 'A man's gotta right to protect what's his.'

Tom rose slowly from his chair and placed a restraining hand on his shoulder. 'You ain't goin' nowhere,' he said calmly. 'You're a farmer. You know 'bout cows an' horses an' how to till a field. But ya don't know nothin' about the type of *hombres* you'll be dealin' with. Or how to stop from being killed.'

The man gazed at him with unwavering eyes. 'It's my job to protect my family,' he said simply. 'An' I mean to do it. This ain't your responsibility. You've done more than could be expected.'

He pulled away and walked over to the wall where a rifle hung on wooden pegs. 'I know how to use this. I don't aim to shoot nobody with it unless I have to but those skunks attacked my family an' thought to see me swing on the end of a rope.' He blew the dust from the old gun.

Tom shrugged, accepting that the older man had a point. The code of the West demanded retribution. But he knew that the men he intended to confront could turn out to be hard, professional gunmen who would have no hesitation in shooting to kill. More than likely they would enjoy it. And what purpose would that serve?

He looked at Dave's hands, working hands, powerful hands that could rope a steer, tame a horse, build a barn, handle a plough. But could he use a handgun if the need arose for lightning-fast action? And Tom was certain that such speed might be necessary.

He searched for a better argument. 'Best you stay with yer family in case there's any more of those snakes around,' he said. 'I was headin' fer town myself. After I've dropped Billy off I'll call in on the marshal, give him a chance to earn his pay.'

Dave shook his head wearily. 'Not much chance there. The marshal don't want trouble. Fact is, he looks the other way, 'tends he's not seen it.'

'That mebbe so,' Tom admitted. 'If he don't take some action then we'll pay a little visit to the rancher. What yer say?'

Dave's wife, who had remained silent for a while and was only now beginning to recover from her ordeal, smiled up at him. 'I wish both of you would just let it go,' she said. 'But I know you won't.' The smile vanished. 'What Tom says makes sense. The law should sort it out.'

Alice spoke softly. 'I was intending to take the buggy into Salvation to get supplies. What if I went with Tom? That is, if he doesn't mind.'

'Great idea,' Tom said, seeing this as the best reason

for keeping her pa at the house. 'I'll see your daughter safely there and back. You have my word on that. I don't reckon you'll have any more trouble here fer a bit but it'd be a good idea to have a man about the place.'

'I didn't do too well last time,' Dave said. 'They took me by surprise.'

'If trouble comes now you'll be ready fer it. Anyway, yer hired help can keep their guns ready.'

'Joe's away till tomorrow,' Dave explained. 'But we'll manage.'

Tom nodded and turned to Alice. 'Ready?'

He led the way outside and retrieved his horse while Alice prepared the buggy. Dave's face was set in grim lines as they wrapped the dead bodies in sheets and secured them on the backs of their horses.

Tom tied the horses to the rear of the buggy and climbed up onto the seat, laying the Winchester under the cover at the back. Billy sat between him and Alice, who held the reins in her hand. 'You don't object to being driven by a woman?' she asked sweetly.

He had no answer to that.

The ride to Salvation took forty minutes but, for Tom, it was over too quickly.

CHAPTER 4

Halfway down the main street Curly Thomson and Lofty Tate hesitated outside the marshal's office, a brick building with a heavy door and barred windows. Their natural instincts were to avoid the law whenever possible but they had served their time, taken their punishment, and now reckoned they were free of any jurisdiction.

During their trial they had kept silent about the involvement of the boy, Tom, not through loyalty but so that the stash of money would not be discovered before they could collect it themselves.

They mounted the steps and pushed open the door. Inside they found Buck Clements seated behind a desk, which was covered with papers.

The marshal, leaning back in his creaking wooden chair, looked up wearily. He was a large man, middle-aged, his eyes deep under bushy brows. 'What kin I do fer you?' he began, then stared at his visitors with dawning recognition. 'Bin a long time,' he said at last. 'Bin enjoying yer holiday?' He grinned.

45

Curly grinned back. 'You've put on a few pounds,' he said. 'Few more grey hairs, too.'

The marshal's expression changed. 'If that's the best insult you kin come up with, git outa my office. On the other hand, if you got any crimes you want to confess to then I'm yer man.' He looked up expectantly. 'I hear there's a few vacancies where ya've just come from.'

Curly grabbed a chair and sat opposite the marshal. Lofty pushed papers aside and perched himself on the corner of the desk.

'Make yerselves comfortable,' Buck Clements grated. 'An' state yer business. I'm a busy man.'

Curly shrugged. 'We're here to offer our help,' he said. 'But if ya don't want it—'

'The last time you did any helping it was to help yerselves to the payroll.'

Lofty nodded. 'That's just it, Marshal. We never did get our hands on that money. Morgan took it an' hid it afore he died. There was a reward on it if I recall.'

The marshal's face split in an enormous grin. 'That's the best fun I've heard in a long time. An' you think you kin find it? Is that what you came here fer? You're out o' luck if you think I'm gonna help ya in that. As fer the reward, if anyone gets it it'll be me.'

'You got it the wrong way round,' Curly said. 'We might be able to help you.'

'I'm listenin', but if yer wasting my time I'm gonna lock you up in one o' my comfortable cells.'

Curly chose his words carefully. 'There was a boy, the nephew of Morgan Jones. He didn't take part in the hold-up. If we could trace him we may get a lead.'

'Name? Have ya gotta name you kin give me?'

'Deegan. Tom Deegan. He lived with his uncle.'

The marshal rose from his chair and opened the door. 'Git outa here. I told you not to waste my time. Think I ain't looked into that? Git.'

The two men left quickly, knowing they would get nothing from the wily marshal.

'I need a drink,' Lofty said.

Slim heard the printing press when he was sixty feet away. The sound came from a building towards the far end of the main street. A sign on the boarding above the open door told him that this was the office of the *Salvation Reporter*.

He stepped inside where a man of about thirty, attired in overalls and with shirtsleeves rolled up, was bent over a printing press. Slim went over and tapped the man on the shoulder.

'What the. . . .' The man jerked erect. He was fresh-faced with short, greying hair. His smile of welcome faded as he took note of his visitor.

'Need some information,' Slim shouted without pre-amble.

'You could've bin more . . .' the man began, but stopped short when he looked into eyes that held in their depths something dark and menacing. 'What sort of help?'

'What's yer name?'

'Bill Bentley.'

'How long's this paper bin around?'

The man turned off the press and wiped his hands

on some rag. 'Nigh on twenty years,' he said proudly. 'My pa started it then. Jus' one sheet of news. I've built it up an' now it's read as far away as—'

'Thirteen years ago,' Slim interrupted, 'the stage was held up and men got killed. You'd've reported that, I guess.'

'Remember it well. Bad day that was. A woman passenger, four men and a boy shot down in cold blood. The leader of the gang an' one o' the outlaws died but the other two spent some time in prison.'

'I know all that,' Slim said, coldly. 'Got any back numbers I can look at?'

'Keep copies of everythin',' Bill told him proudly. He went into the back room and, while Slim waited, sorted through piles of newsprint. 'Here we are.' He brought out an armful of papers. 'You'll find everythin' you need there.'

Slim swept papers off a small table by the window and laid out the bundle. He soon found what he wanted, a headline from a paper dated 10 June 1866.

MASSACRE AT NESTERS' CREEK

The stagecoach, on its way to the town of Salvation, was held up by outlaws who shot and killed two guards, the driver and two passengers, a man and a woman, who were on their way to begin a new life in the West. Also shot down in cold blood was a young man, the son of a local farmer, apparently out riding and by chance arriving at the scene at the wrong time. It was not known how many outlaws were involved. Although the same

bunch has been responsible for several other acts
of violence in the area, this was by far the worst.
The stagecoach was carrying a large sum of money
bound for the bank. Marshal Brady has enlisted
the help of the law from nearby towns and has
promised that he will track the killers down to
make them pay for their crimes. A reward has
been offered for the return of the money and the
arrest and conviction of the killers.

Slim, aware that he was being watched, read on.
When the report mentioned the sum of money
involved he drew in a deep breath, skipped the rest and
turned to future issues of the paper until he came upon
something that held his interest.

ARREST OF OUTLAW GANG

Due to the tireless efforts of our marshal two men
have been found guilty of the stagecoach hold-up
at Nesters' Creek in June.

A posse, headed by the marshal and the county
sheriff, tracked down the outlaws and captured
them without casualties. It is known that the
leader of the gang, now identified as Morgan
Jones the well-respected preacher, received
gunshot wounds during the hold-up and died
from his injuries.

The preacher's nephew, 16-year-old Tom
Deegan, has told this newspaper how he came
upon the stagecoach shortly after the hold-up. It
seems that, at great risk to himself, he released the

team of horses from the blazing coach and
rescued a small child who had been in danger of
being burned to death. The money has so far not
been found.

Slim smiled to himself. 'I reckon Wells Fargo had
more to do with the capture of them outlaws than ever
the marshal did,' he muttered. He was not impressed
with the law in Salvation.

Without another word he left the office, the name
Tom Deegan in his mind.

Another half-hour, with the shadows of the tall pines
lining the trail pointing east, Tom saw the town of
Salvation ahead of them. Alice had been an interesting
and vivacious companion. During the ride Tom had
studied her with unconcealed admiration, noticing the
way her hair framed her face, how her delicate fingers
held the reins, and the movement of her slender body
with the motion of the buggy.

Tom directed them to the front of a clothing store.
He laid his hand on Billy's shoulder. 'This is where you
get off,' he said. 'Aunt Jane's expecting you.'

As he spoke, the door of the shop opened and his
aunt stood there with a smile of welcome. She was
dressed smartly in a long floral dress.

Her smile froze when she saw the bodies draped over
the saddles. 'You've brought trouble with you,' she said.

'You could say that,' Tom agreed. 'I'll tell you everything later. But we have some important business to talk
over with the marshal.'

Jane acknowledged Alice and turned her attention to Billy. 'Hi, Billy,' she said. 'You'll be staying with me for a few days. That'll be nice, won't it? Later you kin take yer horse down to the livery. OK?'

Billy grimaced, not happy with the arrangements.

Tom pressed coins into his son's hand. 'You'll need to pay yer keep.' Billy looked at his pa, then, without speaking, jumped down from the buggy.

Tom followed. 'Mebbe you'll be able to make yerself useful in your aunt's store,' he said. 'An' mebbe show yer aunt how well ya kin cook,' he added, hoping to make Billy smile.

As Billy disappeared into the cool interior of the shop, Tom walked over to his aunt. 'Thanks, Jane,' he said. 'I owe yer.'

'You always did,' Jane said. 'But this can only be for a short while. I've a busy life now. A widow has to work hard to make a living.'

'I wouldn't've asked but I have to keep him safe. And he knows you. It won't be too difficult fer him, 'specially as you brought him up fer four years.'

'You've let him run wild since then, wild and head-strong. He needs a mother's firm hand.' Jane glanced up at Alice, who had remained on the buggy. She smiled. 'You'd make a good couple.'

'None of your business,' Tom said. He kissed her on the cheek, climbed up next to Alice and they moved away.

They hitched the buggy and horses at the rail outside the law office and mounted the three steps to the boardwalk.

51

Tom didn't bother to knock and the marshal was caught off-guard pouring himself a good measure of whiskey into a tin mug. He looked up, angry at the second interruption in a short time. Tom studied him, thinking that mebbe the lawman was running to fat.

'There're two dead bodies outside,' Tom said without preamble. 'Two shooters attacked Dave Green's house, scared his family an' tried to lynch him.'

'Looks like they didn't succeed,' the marshal said without emotion.

'Seems they didn't,' Tom agreed. 'What're ya gonna do about it?' The marshal's indifference angered him but he held himself in check.

'What's your part in all this?'

'I happened to be passin',' Tom said, pushing a chair forward for Alice to sit down while he sat on the corner of the desk. 'Don't agree with lynching. I'd've thought that wouldn't be your idea o' justice.'

'It ain't,' Clements said. 'But I don't like dead bodies, neither. Did you do the shooting?'

'Yep.'

'Any witnesses?'

Alice leaned forward. 'My family were all there,' she said. 'We're alive because of this man. Shooting in self-defence is allowable by law, I believe.'

The sarcasm in her voice seemed to rile the marshal. 'Yeah. OK. No cause to git sassy. I'll see if I kin recognize those *hombres* an' mebbe take it from there.'

'I know where they're from,' Alice said. 'The Triple O ranch.'

'I said I'd deal with it. Now, I've had a busy day.' The

marshal looked at Tom. 'You're Tom Deegan, ain't ya?'

'What of it?'

'Just had two men askin' about ya. What's that all about?'

Tom's eyes widened. He knew without being told. 'What did they want?'

'I'm askin' the questions. If I told you the men were Curly Thomson and Lofty Tate what would ya say?'

'I'd say they're nothin' to do with me.'

'Now why would they be askin' after you?'

'I don't know. What did ya tell them?'

Instead of answering Tom's question, the marshal said, 'Morgan Jones was yer uncle, weren't he?'

'What of it?'

'You rode with him an' his gang, didn't ya?'

'Not exactly. He was a hard man. He said he was trying to bring me up to be tough, s'all.'

The marshal apparently found this funny. 'I guess you didn't get any of the money they robbed and killed fer, then.'

When Tom made no reply he said, 'The money from their last hold-up was never recovered. Would you know anythin' about that?'

Tom didn't like the way the conversation was going.

'We came in to tell you about a crime,' he said, 'expecting you to do somethin' about it. That's what law officers are s'posed to do, ain't it?'

The marshal was showing signs of annoyance. 'Those two rattlesnakes, and yer uncle as well, killed six people when they held up that stagecoach. They think because they served thirteen years in—'

He broke off as Alice leaped to her feet. Her face was white, her fists clenched. 'One of those who were murdered by that gang was my brother,' she hissed, having difficulty getting the words out. 'He wasn't even on the coach, just passing, and they gunned him down, just seventeen.'

Tom looked at her in horror, seeing in her eyes the dawning of recognition of his own involvement.

But that wasn't Alice's immediate concern. 'I want to talk to those men,' she said. 'Where are they?'

'I wouldn't advise that,' the marshal said. 'They're dangerous. Best let it go.'

Alice was having none of it. 'Where will they be?'

'More'n likely fillin' themselves up with liquor,' Tom told her. 'An' that's no place fer a woman.'

'Think I haven't seen the inside of a saloon before?' she said and, before either man could stop her, she had pulled the door open and stomped outside.

Tom rose to his feet and followed. 'Wait!' he cried.

Buck Clements shrugged and stayed where he was.

CHAPTER 5

Curly Thomson and Lofty Tate were satisfying their thirst, both smarting at the reception given to them by Buck Clements. The more they drank the more their annoyance coloured their conversation.

Lofty glanced over at the gaming tables. 'I'm gonna see what I kin take off them varmints.'

'Please yerself,' Curly said, knowing that his partner, in spite of the liquor he had consumed, would easily fleece the hicks who were playing there. And they badly needed the money. 'I'll stay here a piece,' he said.

Standing where he was he could watch Lofty's back in case of trouble. He'd decided there was time enough after they'd found the loot to get rid of him. Right now there was something he had to do. Something had been picking at the corners of his mind, an idea that had been festering for some time. Reaching a decision he took his glass and sauntered slowly over to stand near the tall man at the end of the counter.

Curly watched as Slim took a cigar from his pocket and placed it in his mouth. Curly took his opportunity.

He struck a match and held it out.

'Prefer to light my own,' the man grated and struck a Vesta with his thumb. Through the smoke he turned his cold stare at Curly, who was still holding the flaming match.

'Name's Thomson,' Curly said. 'Friends call me Curly.'

Slim drew deeply on his cigar. 'An' what do yer enemies call ya?'

Curly grinned. 'Often they don't last long enough to call me anythin' at all.'

His hand hovered close to his hip where a six-gun hung in its holster. 'I've seen yer watching us. Me and my pard. Fact is, yer've bin followin' us. Now, why would anyone wanna do that?'

Slim's eyes narrowed, giving Curly a hard look. 'I can mebbe think of one.'

'An' what would that be?'

'Cain't talk here. Best go outside.'

Curly glanced around the room. He shook his head vigorously. 'Nope, we talk here.'

Slim leaned forward and spoke softly in Curly's ear. 'You want all these men to hear the magic words?' he whispered.

Curly's mouth dropped open. He closed it quickly. 'That'd keep a man in luxury fer the rest of his life.'

'You lookin' to do that?' Slim asked.

'What's that to you?'

Slim shrugged. 'I didn't want you to be disappointed, that's all.'

'I don't intend to be.'

'Best be prepared in case.'

'Case of what?'

'Case ya might run into trouble,' Slim said, the trace of a smile appearing on his lips.

Curly wondered if he could outdraw this infuriating man. Whoever he was he knew more than was good for him. 'Who are ya?'

'They call me Slim. You could look on me as a friend,' Slim said. 'Friends give advice an' I've got some fer you.'

'What would that be?'

Slim's face creased into smile. 'Why, give up on what you came here fer. Let someone else take over afore you get hurt.'

'Sounds like a threat.'

'Take it how you like. It's good advice.'

'Think I'll pass.'

'Well, you've bin warned.'

'OK. But if yer reckoning to do anythin' but talk you'd best be good with that pistol o' yourn.'

'Not received many complaints on that score.' Slim casually withdrew one of the Colts and thrust it into Curly's belly. 'I don't have to be fast. All I gotta do is pull the trigger.'

Curly didn't blink. 'Not in here you won't.' He raised his hands to shoulder level. 'See, you'd be shootin' a man who hadn't drawn on yer. Agin the law, that is.'

'So it is,' Slim smirked. 'I'd quite forgotten. Then again, you'd not be alive to tell the tale.' He re-holstered his weapon. 'Now, are we gonna talk somewhere private? Outside, mebbe?'

Curly pondered his options. He needed to know what this man knew and what he intended to do with the information. He was clearly informed about the money but he'd hardly be standing at the bar if he knew where it was.

Curly judged that, from the look of the man, the way he stood like a coiled spring and the manner in which he wore his Colt, he was not a man that he could outdraw. Going outside would not be a clever thing to do. He would have to use cunning to rid them of this unexpected nuisance.

'I need to talk to my pard,' he said. He glanced round at the tables and noticed that Lofty had linked arms with one of the saloon ladies and was accompanying her up the wooden stairs. So much for topping up their bank balance.

On a sudden impulse he quickly turned on his heel. Any further discussion with Slim could wait. He waved away one of the doves who had sidled up to him. Thirteen long years without female company had ignited deep urges, but, although his desires were not yet satisfied, he had other urgent matters on his mind.

He felt cold eyes on his back as he went up the stairs. He heard Lofty's voice through the bedroom door, sounding as though he was making the most of his recreational activities.

'Can't worry 'bout that,' he muttered and pushed the door open without knocking. Lofty looked up, the girl screamed.

'We gotta get going soon,' Curly said. 'Give ya thirty minutes. Either ya ready or I go without ya.'

While he waited he stood on the balcony and watched with interest the scene being enacted below.

All the while he stood there his mind wouldn't let go of the notion that the stranger posed a threat and that he and Lofty should do something about it.

Perhaps the best thing they could do would be to act swiftly to find out where the loot had been stashed. If Slim, as he had called himself, was chasing the same prize then he and Lofty had to stay a step in front. Tom Deegan seemed to be the key. An early call on that snake-in-the-grass might be useful.

Tom had caught up with Alice before she had gone more than a few steps. He held her shoulder and swung her round. 'What d'ya think you're gonna do?' He was conscious of the slender flesh beneath his fingers.

Alice pulled clear. 'I'm going to tell them, those . . . those men, what they did to my family. I want to see their faces. If I was a man I'd want to kill them for what they did.'

'But you're a woman,' Tom said, 'an' you're not equipped to confront such men.'

Alice bridled. 'Yes, I am a woman, as you so quaintly put it. D'you think you're that much better just because you're stronger and wear a gun?'

'I didn't mean no offence,' Tom said quickly. 'All I'm sayin' is those *hombres* in the saloon'll be all fired up with liquor an' won't take kindly to bein' confronted by a woman.'

Alice kept walking but her pace had slowed. 'Those men, they think because they've served their time. . . . If

Pa gets to know they're here I'm not sure what he'd do.' She stopped and pain showed in her eyes.

Tom turned to her. 'We can't let that happen. They'd shoot him down afore he got within speaking distance.'

When they reached the entrance to the saloon Alice's bravado had lessened although her intentions were the same. 'I wouldn't mind if you came in with me,' she said.

'I've gotta better idea,' Tom said. 'You stay here. I'll see how it is in there an' I'll come out and tell you. Then, if you're still of a mind. . . .'

Alice nodded. Tom guided her a few steps safely away along the boardwalk, pushed through the batwings and assessed the possibilities. His gaze swept around, looking for the two men whom he had last seen more than thirteen years ago, not sure whether he would recognize them again. Would they recognize him?

Although there were many faces he knew, and some he did not, he saw no one resembling Curly or Lofty. He was about to leave when Alice was pulled brutally into the saloon by a large cowpoke, who was already showing signs of overindulgence. Alice struggled in his grip.

'Look what I found,' the man roared. 'Waitin' fer me, she was.'

Tom pivoted. 'Let her go,' he growled.

The man guffawed. 'You kin have her when I'm finished.'

Tom grasped the man's arm, felt the iron-hard muscle beneath the shirt. The man was not only big, he was powerful, and Tom was to discover he was fast, too, a combination hard to beat. But his own muscles were strong, built up by years of hard work, and his fingers dug in.

Alice was forgotten and she stood with her hand up to her mouth, unable to help.

Tom saw the fist coming, but too late. Although he tried to swing out of the way the vicious punch, intended for his head, struck him hard on the shoulder. The force of the blow spun him round, twisting his head on his neck. His assailant's attack was disciplined with the clear intention of finishing the fight almost before it had begun.

And he almost did it. Tom knew he would have to be quicker but, as he recovered, the man followed up his early success with two more lightning strikes that sent Tom staggering backwards.

Through his swimming senses he heard a voice call out, 'Go fer it, Wolf. That's Tom Deegan. He just brung two of our men in. Dead.'

Wolf needed no encouragement. He came in for the kill.

Tom struggled to keep his balance but a foot, stuck out deliberately behind him, brought him crashing to the floor. Wolf, with a wide grin stretching his mouth, swaggered up to him and drew back his foot.

Even stretched out on the floor Tom was far from helpless. He saw the boot from the corner of his eye, rolled, drew back his foot and, with all the considerable strength he possessed kicked at Wolf's kneecap. He heard something crack and was rewarded with a wild cry of rage and pain from his assailant.

As he sprang to his feet he twisted round to confront the owner of the foot that had tripped him. Without pausing he unleashed a savage left hook to the jaw with all the weight of his body behind it. The man was rocked back against the bar and was unconscious even before he hit the floor, a look of surprise still set on his face.

But now Wolf was coming at him again and there was an expression in his eyes that spoke of murder. This time his attack was not so controlled. Tom had time to avoid the on-rush and to come back with a series of well-timed and accurate punches to head and body.

The man was solid muscle – that much was clear – but even powerful muscle can feel pain. Wolf took several steps back and Tom took full advantage of his opponent's temporary retreat. He bore in with both arms working like pistons, driving Wolf back until he could go no further.

There, because he could no longer retreat, Wolf made a stand. Although his punches were ill-controlled, some landed where they were intended. Tom felt an iron fist sink into his midriff and the air exploded from his lungs. He doubled up, gasping, and took several quick steps back, trying to distance himself from the whirlwind of blows that followed him.

There were cheers from some of the men as Wolf bore down. Tom continued on his backward path, pretending now to be more wounded than he was. Wolf, believing he could deliver the final strike, had dropped his guard.

Tom straightened. He was hurting and knew he

could not continue taking punishment like this. It was now or never. He gathered all his remaining strength and unleashed a double-handed strike to the jaw that ended the fight. Wolf sank first to his knees, then flat on the floor, his eyes glazed.

There was silence for the time it takes to swallow a finger of whiskey, then voices started up together. Someone took hold of Tom's sleeve. 'Best git goin' while ya still can.'

Tom turned to see a tall, slim man with a gun in his hand. But it was not pointed in his direction. It was trained on the two men at the bar who had been shouting encouragement to Wolf. Their hands were dangerously close to their holsters.

'I need to face those men,' Tom said.

'Don't recommend it,' the man said. 'I'll hold them here fer a few minutes until you get yerself an' the lady outa the way. Don't want more dead bodies today.'

Tom nodded. 'It'll keep.'

'Git going.'

'You coming?'

'I ain't finished my drink. They won't trouble me none.'

Tom didn't doubt it. 'Who are ya?'

'Name's Slim.'

'Where're ya staying?'

'Hotel.'

'I'll call in on ya. Much obliged.'

He grabbed Alice's hand and left through the batwings. He rubbed his knuckles. He turned once, feeling the venomous glares piercing his back, then he was out into the fading light. Much as it went against his nature he knew it was time to withdraw, although he guessed the matter was far from ended.

'Think we'd best get you back home,' he said.

Slim Newman returned to his place at the bar and stood with his foot resting on the rail. Hostile eyes followed his movements but no one challenged him. His glass stood untouched on the counter where he had left it. He drained it and signalled for another.

His presence seemed to deter others from starting up a conversation with him. He was aware of this and was used to it. Without appearing to, he had taken note of all the other occupants of the saloon – there was a fair number at this time of day – and had assessed them with the skill of a professional gunman.

He concluded that most were there only for liquor, women and gambling and posed no threat. Three others, including Wolf, who was finding it difficult to nurse his injured pride, damaged knee and broken jaw, were men to be watched.

A girl, he guessed no more than nineteen, slipped up beside him. She was still pretty but the smoke and the job she was employed to do had had the effect of creating lines about her eyes and mouth that made her look older. She smiled, red lips parting to show even teeth.

Slim pushed her away. He enjoyed the attentions of women like any man but only when the time was right and it would be his choice. Now was not the time, not when he was chasing a fortune. No one else approached him, not even the barkeep unless he was summoned.

Slim's attention was drawn to a particular table where one man of about forty-five, dressed elegantly in white silk shirt and long, tailored jacket, seemed to be enjoying the run of the cards. A younger man wearing a check shirt seated at the same table appeared to be upset at consistently losing.

The young man, with a wild look in his eyes, shoved back his chair, leaped to his feet and drew his sleeve across his face. With an air of desperation he shouted, 'Nobody can have that much luck!'

The older man hardly blinked. 'You'd best spell that out,' he said quietly but his voice, soft though it was, carried a threat with it.

'You goddamn know what I mean. You're a cheat. You've cleaned me out. You're a low-down cheat.'

The word, rarely heard but often thought, stunned everyone to silence. Once uttered it could not easily be withdrawn. And the young man clearly had no intention of withdrawing it. There was a gun in his hand and he waved it ominously.

Onlookers, carefully withdrawing from the possible line of fire, waited to see what the older man's response would be. It was not long in coming. He eased his chair back and rose slowly to face his challenger. A silver-handled Colt was hanging in a holster cross-wise by his side.

Neither man had a chance to use their weapons. Slim had moved across the floor on feet as silent as a cat's and now stood between the two men, facing the fancy dresser. His gaze held the man's own as he closed the distance between them and, with a speed that dazzled the eye, he reached forward, withdrew the man's gun and sliced the barrel hard across his head.

The gambler went down without a sound. With the toe of his boot Slim flipped the man's coat aside. Two aces fell face up on the floor.

The young man lost no time in gathering up the dollar bills and stuffing them in his pockets. 'Thanks, mister,' he said. 'I'm mightily obliged fer the help.'

Slim looked hard at him. 'Don't git the wrong idea, son. I weren't helpin' you. If yer old enough to gamble you oughta be prepared to look after yerself.'

As men lifted the still unconscious man into a chair Slim turned away and strolled back to his place at the bar. The young dove came up to him again, admiration in her eyes. 'That was a good thing you done there,' she said. 'That card-sharp's bin asking for that for some time.'

He smiled down at her. 'What I said jus' now still stands. It's just I gotta dislike o' them that cheat at cards, s'all.' He recognized, even as he said it, that this was a weakness in his character but he had seen, when he was only twelve years old, how his own pa had been robbed at the card tables and driven to suicide. He had harboured hatred since then. 'Now, if you've no objection, I'd like to finish my drink in peace.'

Seeing there was no profit to be made here, the girl moved away.

Slim was pleased with the progress he had made with such little effort. Two good deeds in the space of an hour might give the men in the saloon the wrong impression of him, misunderstanding his motives.

Best of it was he'd thrown a scare into the two outlaws, deliberately allowing them to see that he was following them with a view to taking the money for himself. Perhaps that would cause them to hasten their own plans, make them careless. He would send them to Boot Hill later when the time was right.

Even better still, he had recognized the name of Tom Deegan and had earned his gratitude. Perhaps this was the man who could lead him to the hidden loot. If so the future for Curly and his partner was looking poor.

Yes, altogether it had been a good day although not everyone in the room appreciated his actions.

Quite the opposite.

He drank his whiskey, savouring the aftertaste, and walked casually from the saloon, fully aware of the hostile eyes that followed his progress.

He was aware also that it wasn't just eyes that followed him. Two men had come out of the batwings only a few heartbeats after he had left. He allowed them to follow for a short distance, reasoning that they wouldn't want to shoot him in the back while there were folk to witness.

They would surely call him out. He smiled at the thought. After he had disposed of them he could take a ride out to Deegan's place. Just before sunup might be the best time. He would soon be a rich man.

Anticipation of the shoot-out excited him. He'd killed many times before and each time the build-up of tension became more pleasurable. At first, his hatred for killers and the breed of men who enjoyed dealing out death had been enough to drive him on. Then, gradually, he had come to revel in the thrill of the hunt, the confrontation and the fear in the eyes of men as they faced death from his lethal gun.

But the hairs on the back of his neck were bristling as he heard a shout of warning given by the young man in the check shirt. He could leave it no longer. He swivelled on one heel, crouched and waited.

CHAPTER 6

From his vantage point on the balcony of the saloon Curly could see the danger Tom was in although he hadn't recognized who he was until he heard the name.

'Well, well,' he muttered. 'So we've caught up with you at last.'

Although he enjoyed the fight that followed he was prepared to interfere if Tom's life was in danger, reasoning that if he happened to be killed his secret would die with him.

The presence of the girl was interesting. 'Mebbe a little pressure on you would be enjoyable,' he thought. And might make Tom willing to talk. He stored the information away for later.

When Slim stepped into the action, Curly wondered again where the man fitted in. He was pleased to see two men follow him out of the saloon with their intentions clear on their faces. Perhaps he and Lofty wouldn't have to worry about the slim man for too much longer.

He quickly followed other men out through the batwings and onto the boardwalk just in time to see the two gunmen lying motionless in the dirt and Slim holding a smoking gun. He considered putting a slug in Slim right there and then but thought better of it as crowds began to gather.

He returned to the saloon, grabbed Lofty as soon as his partner appeared and told him what he'd seen and heard.

'We're goin' out to Deegan's place. Gonna be there soon as it's light. If he's there we'll loosen his tongue. If he ain't we'll search the place. Grab some sleep.'

But Lofty had better plans for the rest of the night.

Billy, with his face pressed hard against the glass of his Aunt Jane's shop window, had followed the activity taking place in the street outside. He had seen his pa go into the marshal's office then walk over to the saloon.

He had watched, with his heart pounding, as Alice had been roughly dragged through the batwings and, later, how she and his pa had hurried out and quickly driven off in the buggy.

'What's so interesting out there, Billy?' Aunt Jane called.

'Nothin' much,' Billy replied.

He waited. Then he saw Slim. With the instinct of the young he recognized the danger represented by this man and made no move from his position.

He watched Slim walk casually along the street, then took a breath and held it as he saw two men slip from the saloon and follow. The way they moved together, keeping to the shadows, maintaining the distance between them, was unnatural unless they were stalking.

It appeared to Billy that Slim was unaware of their presence. He wanted to call out but it soon became clear that that wasn't necessary when he saw Slim smile and heard a shout of warning.

'I need you to give me a hand, Billy,' Aunt Jane said, coming over to look out the window. 'That is, if you can drag yourself away. . . .' Her voice trailed off as she saw what was happening.

Slim had turned and stood easy, seeming relaxed but ready for action. The two men stopped, taken by surprise by the sudden change.

They called out something that Billy couldn't hear and their hands dropped to their holsters in a blur of movement. But, fast as they were, Slim was faster. Before their gun barrels had risen high enough, Slim's Colt barked twice.

Billy gasped. He had never seen anything like it before and could hardly believe it now. The two men took a step back as the slugs hit them in the chest, then they slowly sagged and lay still in the dust of the street. Slim calmly re-holstered his gun, nodded to the young man in the check shirt, sauntered up to the dead men and spat on their bodies.

By this time folk had gathered round and were telling each other excitedly what they had seen or thought they had seen. Buck Clements strode up the street and pushed his way in, firing questions at anyone who would listen.

'That's not for you to look at, Billy,' Aunt Jane said faintly, clearly upset by what had occurred. She took hold of his shoulder and gently steered him away from

71

the window. 'Now, are you going to help me or not?'

Billy's thoughts were in turmoil. It seemed obvious to his young mind that his pa was in danger, that what he had witnessed a few minutes ago had something to do with it and that the man who had just handled his guns so lethally was a threat to his pa and Alice. Why otherwise would they have driven off in such a hurry?

He visualized his pa alone at the homestead and every instinct told him that he should be there to help. He was nearly a man – almost fourteen years old – and could handle a weapon or keep watch if necessary.

'What sort of trouble's Pa in?' he asked his aunt as she put him to work sorting, tidying and stacking.

'He didn't tell me,' she said. 'But there's no need for you to worry. He wanted to know you were safe and that's why you're here. I'm quite sure he'll be able to look after himself.'

Her words, intended to comfort him, had the opposite effect. Quite sure? What did that mean? And if he, Billy, was safe here did that mean his pa was unsafe at home?

'He needs me,' he said simply. 'Dammit, I've gotta go home.'

'Billy! Your language! No, you're not going anywhere. I promised your pa I'd take care of you and that's what I'm doing. Now, if we don't get a move on we'll be here all night. It's time we went home for supper.'

Billy was not intending to be in town any longer than he could help.

With no more customers entering the shop, Jane

72

tidied up and locked the door. 'Let's go home,' she said, 'and cook ourselves a nice meal. What do you fancy?'

'Anythin',' Billy said. Then, when he realized this would not endear him to his aunt, he added, 'Your cooking's better'n my pa's.'

They left the shop by the back door and walked round to the front. Jane kept her eyes averted from the blood that stained the dirt further up the street. The bodies had been removed but there was still a knot of folk who found it all interesting enough to hang about for.

The light was fading although few stars were yet visible. Billy put on his coat. 'I need to check Tina at the livery,' he said. 'You go on ahead.' He didn't like the idea of lying to his Aunt Jane but there was no other way.

His aunt hesitated as though she was about to dis-agree. 'All right, but make sure you come directly home. I'll be waiting.' Her small house was only ten minutes' walk away at the far end of town and he had been there many times.

Billy walked towards the livery, glancing behind him to make sure his aunt was doing as she said. He waved. Suddenly he caught his breath as he saw the marshal and the shooter making their way along the boardwalk and entering the marshal's office. He waited.

Having seen the tall man in action Billy's curiosity was aroused. When the law office door closed with the men inside he went across the street and crouched under an open window, oblivious to the stares of

THE PREACHER'S LEGACY

anyone watching. From there he could just hear most
of what was being said.

As he listened his heart pounded. Now there was no
doubt in his mind that his pa needed him.

The slim man was saying, 'Self-defence. Enough witnesses to fill a church.'

'Yeah, I know,' the marshal said. 'I heard folk talkin'.
Somethin' 'bout a gambler.'

'Word gets round fast, don't it?'

'Yep. Seems like yer've made some friends an' some
enemies at the same time. Tell me what happened.'

'Two varmints thought they'd take me. They made a
bad mistake.'

'So it'd seem.'

'What else kin I tell ya?'

'You kin start by telling me why they'd wanna do
that.'

Billy heard a match strike and he caught the whiff of
cigar smoke.

'Cain't rightly say,' the man said. 'Mebbe friends o'
the card-sharp. Mebbe somethin' to do with a man
likely to've bin shot if I hadn't bin there.'

'Did he have a name, this man?'

'Yeah, I heard 'em call him Tom Deegan. Somethin'
like that, anyway.'

There was silence for a while, then, 'Interesting,' the
marshal said. 'Same young man as brought in two dead
bodies earlier on today.'

'So I unnerstand.'

'Four dead men in as many hours. Would there be a
connection, d'ya reckon?'

'Dunno. You're the law. You figure it out.'

Billy sensed a sharpness entering the marshal's voice. 'Yep, I'm the law an' I'm gonna figure this out. What's the connection twixt you and this Tom Deegan?'

'We jus' met. He had to hurry away so we didn't git properly acquainted.' Billy heard the scraping of a chair as it was pushed back and he prepared to run. The marshal continued, 'I don't b'lieve in coincidences. No more do I think you're tellin' me all you know. Not thinkin' of leaving town fer a while, are ya?'

'Not fer a day or so, Marshal. I'm stayin' at the big hotel. Why'd yer wanna know?'

'You're real handy with a gun.'

'What's that mean?'

'How'd yer like to apply to be deputy marshal here?'

'What happened to the last man?'

'He got hisself killed.'

Both men laughed.

'I'll think on it.'

'You do that. Meantime I gotta hankerin' to speak to Deegan some more afore I question you again.'

'I'd like to renew my acquaintance with him myself. P'raps you could tell me where he hangs out. I'll drop by and have a chat.'

'No objection to that,' the marshal said. 'You could save me a trip out. Tell him I wanna see him. Will you do that?'

'No trouble at all.'

'OK. He's gotta small farm up beyond Cooper's Bluff. Forty-minute ride. I b'lieve he has a son, a boy of about thirteen or so.'

'Great,' the man said. 'I'm very fond o' children.'

Billy had been there long enough. Not only did he need to give his pa support, he had to warn him of what the slim man had said.

He hurried away to collect his horse, thinking quickly. He patted her neck and whispered in her ear. 'Sorry, Tina, but you gotta take me home. Plenty of food an' rest when we get there.'

But he had a problem. His aunt would be worried and would be looking for him when he failed to turn up. He looked around and recognized a boy of about his own age. He beckoned frantically and the boy came over. 'Ben, I need you to do somethin' fer me.'

'I'm late back already,' Ben said.

Billy searched in his pockets for the money his pa had given him to pay his way. 'Won't take a minute. Silver dollar fer you if you promise to do it.'

Ben's eyes opened wide. 'Want me to kill someone?'

'Nothin' like that,' Billy told him without smiling. 'You know where my Aunt Jane lives, don'tcha? Well, all you gotta do is go there now and tell her I won't be back tonight. I'm goin' home. Will ya tell her that?'

'Fer a dollar I'll tell her anything.' Ben held out his hand and closed it swiftly over the hard metal as he ran off to take the message.

Billy didn't hesitate. He saddled the bay and set his mount off at a steady pace.

He was on his way home. Although it would be dark before he arrived he would be on very familiar territory.

CHAPTER 7

Alice had felt the strength in Tom's hand as he guided her out through the batwings. Yet she sensed a gentleness there, too, and allowed her hand to remain in his for longer than was necessary.

She acknowledged to herself that she had been terrified while she had been dragged into the saloon and as she stood powerless, watching the progression of the fight between Tom and Wolf. Her pretence at bravado might have fooled some but she knew that, if it hadn't been for the intervention of the slim man, she may not have got out of the saloon so easily.

She was still shaking as they stepped up into the buggy and moved out quickly.

'Are you hurt bad?' she asked, noticing that Tom was having some difficulty.

'Had worse,' he said.

'D'you know who that man was?'

'The one who helped us? No, can't say as I do but he was useful to have around.'

'So are you. You got into a fight on account of me.'

'I did what any man would've done.' Her gratitude seemed to mean a lot to him. 'Mebbe I'll make a point of visitin' him tomorrow. Same time I kin look in on Billy, see how he's gettin' on with Aunt Jane.

'I don't cotton to the idea of running away but I gave my word to ya pa I'd see ya back safe. I mean to keep that promise. I need to settle matters with those men in the saloon but for now the important thing is to get you home.'

Alice nodded. She felt grateful that he'd not offered any criticism over her determination to enter the saloon and the dangerous situation that it had led to. It had been a silly notion that could have ended badly.

As it was she noticed that Tom was continually scanning their back trail. 'Do you think they'll follow us?' she asked.

Tom sounded confident. 'Nope. Don't reckon so. More likely to go fer the slim man but, from the look of him, seems he's more'n capable of taking care o' himself.'

They continued at a good pace. The light had now faded, making it difficult to distinguish shadow from form. Alice found herself admiring Tom's profile as she rode silently beside him, her hands clenched tight on the reins. She waited for him to speak.

Eventually he broke the silence. 'I'm sorry you had to go through that back there.'

Alice managed a smile. 'You warned me, but I wanted to see those two men, the ones who robbed the stage and killed my brother. There's so much I don't understand; how men can shoot a boy out of the saddle;

how they feel they have the right to rob and murder.'

'They were outlaws, pure and simple. There's no reasoning behind their actions.'

'The marshal said they were asking about you?' It was a question rather than a statement.

Tom didn't answer immediately. 'Yeah, I told him I didn't know why.'

She knew, with a woman's intuition, that he was concealing the truth, could recognize it by the tone of his voice, the way he turned away from her.

They rode on in silence again, relaxing as the faint orange glow to the west faded and the stars made their appearance in the darkening sky like holes in black velvet.

Alice felt a warmth towards the man who now rode by her side. Yet there was a gulf between them, too, something to do with his past, perhaps, and the two outlaws in the saloon.

But for now she was content to let the conversation end. Now the probability of pursuit was no longer a threat she was more relaxed and sensed that Tom felt the same way. They had slowed the horses to walking pace.

Alice, on a sudden impulse, guided the buggy through a stand of willow and entered a clearing where a small creek rippled over its bed of stones, reflecting the rising moon in a thousand lights.

They stepped down, allowing their horses to drink the cool water and eat the lush grass growing along the bank.

Alice felt at peace with the man beside her. But the

moment didn't last.

Tom suddenly turned to face her. 'I haven't told ya the truth. Not the whole of it, anyway. I was there at the hold-up that day. My task was to stash the money so the others could pick it up later.'

Alice felt the blood drain from her face. Suddenly, in those few words, she was seeing Tom in a new light. 'You were a member of the gang?'

'I was sixteen at the time.'

Could he really be offering that as an excuse? 'You took the money?'

'Yeah, but I didn't stash it where I was s'posed to.'

'You used it?' There was cold sarcasm in her voice. 'Was it worth the lives of all those people?'

'I never used it.'

'Was it ever recovered?'

'No.'

'D'you know where it is now?'

His hesitation showed he was not prepared to answer the question. 'It'll probably stay hidden fer a long time,' he told her. 'It's best that way. Mebbe rotted by now.'

Her mood had changed, the death of her brother still an open wound.

Without another word they continued their journey. Alice was glad when they were approaching her house. 'Yer pa'll be pleased to see you,' Tom said.

'Thank you,' she said, but she was angry.

So much had happened in such a short time and she didn't know where it might end. 'You'd best stay the night here,' she said.

'Reckon I'll push on home soon as I've spoken to yer

pa,' he said.

But he was easily persuaded to stay. He was weary, feeling the effects of the bruises and cuts inflicted on him during his fight with Wolf. He readily accepted Dave Green's offer of hospitality.

'Animals'll be fine till morning,' he said. 'And Billy's safe with Aunt Jane.'

Billy rode hard back to his house. The bay responded well. As shadows merged and the way ahead became more difficult to see he slowed down, knowing that a false step could break the horse's leg. To be stranded alone in the dark was not something he liked to think about.

He wasn't so easily able to keep his thoughts away from the slim man he had seen shooting two men down so callously in the street. He had claimed self-defence and no doubt it was, but the lack of emotion in the man's face and the way he spat on the corpses had sent chills down Billy's spine.

The man had said he intended to visit his pa and that fear urged him on. As he approached the house he expected to see some evidence of activity, some light from the windows. There was nothing.

'Pa!' he shouted as he entered the yard and reined in the bay. 'Pa, where are you?'

He could be out with the livestock, he surmised, but quickly realized that was not likely after sundown. The truth was that his pa wasn't here. And if not here, where was he? He went into the cabin and lit a lamp, the yellow light bringing some comfort. He looked around.

Nothing seemed to be out of place and his uneasiness began to leave him.

He fed, watered, rubbed down and settled his own horse and the others in the corral before he heated some soup for himself and broke off a hunk of bread to fill his belly. He was tired and knew he could do nothing more until morning. He lay down fully clothed on his bunk and, within a few minutes, dropped off into a deep but troubled sleep, hoping his pa would return soon.

CHAPTER 8

Tom slept badly, the events of thirteen years ago returning in his dreams. He wished he could turn the clock
back, undo the terrible things he had witnessed on that
day. He had to accept that he could not have influenced
the events and hoped that Alice would come to accept
that, too.

Tomorrow it might all be resolved.

In the morning Tom was glad he had stayed. Over
breakfast of eggs, bacon, bread and coffee, Dave said,
'If Buck Clements fails to carry out the duties he's paid
fer and uphold the law, then I will.'

Tom raised his eyebrows. 'And do exactly what?'

'First, go talk to John Gordon, the big rancher who
b'lieves he's beyond the law. He already owns most of
the good grazing hereabouts and he ain't satisfied with
that. He's driven some of my neighbours away and tried
to turn me and my family off our rightful land. He tried
to kill me. He won't stop now 'less someone makes him.'

'And that's gonna be you?'

'I'll do what I have to do.'

'His ranch is bristlin' with guns.'

Dave grinned. 'He's already missing two.' He dabbed at his lips and turned to his wife. 'And that was a great meal, Mary.'

'You don't get round me that way, Dave,' Mary said. 'I don't want you to do anything silly. Let's just sell up and start someplace else.'

Dave ran his fingers through his hair. 'There's only one person who'll buy this place, and that's John Gordon. His offer is only half what it's worth.' He made an expansive gesture with his arm. 'See, Tom, a man would have to be crazy to give up what we've built up here.'

Tom nodded, thinking for a moment what he himself had given up to maintain a quiet life. 'I'm not suggestin' you give anythin' up. I said I'd go with you an', if you're hog-set on it, I will. We'll see what the big man has to say.'

He wondered how he had so quickly become involved in all this and in doing so, almost forgotten about Curly Thomson and Lofty Tate.

At least, he reassured himself again, Billy was safely away from danger.

John Gordon thumped the solid mahogany table with his fist. 'Four of my men shot down! How in hell did that happen?'

The rancher was a big, impressive man, aged about fifty, six feet tall, broad-shouldered, with black hair sleeked back and greying at the temples. His eyes were dark and hooded. He was dressed in the finest tailored jacket and pants, red shirt secured at the neck with a bow tie.

The room they were in was large and airy, accessed through a wide, carpeted hall. It was richly furnished with mahogany table and upholstered chairs, cabinets, bookshelves, long-case clock and plush curtains. The windows, stretching from wall to wall, provided a panoramic view of the valley and the mountains beyond.

His stood with feet apart, firmly planted on the soft, Persian carpet.

His anger now was directed at the wiry cowhand who stood before him. 'Tell me, Zac. How can that be? I hire the best.'

'I'm only tellin' ya what I know,' Zac said, clearly nervous. 'Don't know nothin' about how Dutch an' Carlos got theirselves carted into town slung over their own hosses.'

'Who brought them in?'

'A homesteader by name of Deegan, so I b'lieve. Didn't see it myself. There was a farmer with him. Dave Green. Seen him around.'

'This Deegan, did the marshal throw him in jail?'

'Nope. That's just it. Deegan seems to've teamed up with a stranger. They was in the saloon an' there was a ruckus. The stranger set about one o' the gamblers an' Deegan put Wolf on the floor.'

'Wolf gets into too many fights.'

'He might regret getting into that one with a busted jaw.'

'Maybe teach him a lesson. But he'll be no good to

me if he's badly hurt.'

'After that Lou an' Joey thought they'd take the stranger down but he shot 'em both. Folk say he's lightnin' fast.'

'I don't care how fast he is. He's human, ain't he? He can die like anyone else.'

'Yeah, boss.'

'And what did Buck Clements do then?'

'Nothin' 'sfar as I could see. I came here fast as I could. Thought you should know.'

'Of course I needed to know. What was your part in all this?'

Zac hesitated. What was expected of him? His boss hired hard men to use their guns, while he was just a cowhand. He was not paid to risk his life in a shoot-out.

'I'm only tellin' ya what I seen,' he repeated, hoping that would be enough.

The rancher stood for a few moments, his fists clenched. 'Go get Seth and Cato. Tell them I want them here right away.' He spat the words out. 'And I want you to ride back into town and tell the marshal I want to speak to him. Now! Whatever he's doing bring him here. Wake him up or sober him up, I don't care. What does he think I'm paying him for? Go!'

Zac appeared to be happy to leave and to carry out the duties assigned to him. He did not like being on the receiving end of the rancher's wrath.

When he had gone the rancher moved over to a large, ornate cabinet, which held a variety of bottles. He poured himself a good measure of pale amber whiskey and stood looking out of the curved window with the crystal glass in his hand.

From there, during the day, it gave him pleasure to gaze over the expanse of his spread to the mountains beyond. Now, in the night, he was looking at his own reflection and was almost as satisfied with that.

By the time Seth and Cato, two of his top guns, arrived, his anger had still not subsided. 'I pay you good money to keep the lid on things. Four men dead and one with a busted jaw. What's going on?'

Neither of the two men were in awe of their paymaster but, while he kept paying, they were happy to show some loyalty.

Seth, the older of the two, had an aggressive manner, which he attempted to control when talking to the rancher. He was a mere five and a half feet tall with cold eyes, a pointed nose and bloodless lips set in a thin face. His voice was soft but that was the only thing gentle about him.

'We should've sent more'n two to deal wi' the farmer but we didn't know he had help. It won't happen next time.'

'And the two in town?'

'I was upstairs in one o' the rooms at the time,' Cato said. 'Di'n't hear a thing.' He was in his early twenties, brash, over-confident, good-looking, a favourite of the doves in the saloon. Now he was far from being apologetic. 'Lou an' Joey should've bin able to deal with any trouble that came their way but I b'lieve they were shot down in cold blood by a stranger.'

'And Wolf?'

'He tangled with a local homesteader an' came off

worse. It won't do him no harm.'

John Gordon was far from satisfied with the explanations he had been given. 'There's something going on here and I want to know what it is. I want you to go into Salvation as soon as it's light, find the men responsible and get rid of them. Take Zac with you. He'll recognize the men you're after.'

'Leave it to us, boss.'

'I don't care how you go about it but I don't want it to become known that I'm involved. Plans are at a delicate stage and I don't want them spoiled now. Four of my best men've been killed already. It's beginning to look as if we're in a war, drawing too much attention to the Triple O. How could that happen?'

'Dunno, boss. It won't happen no more.'

'I expect you to see to it. Seems like the trouble started with Tom Deegan and that goddamn farmer. Then it seems someone else stepped in and worsened things. I reckon life would be a hell of a lot simpler if those three got lost somewhere. Permanently. Can I rely on you to see to that? I pay you enough, don't I? And take more men if you can't handle it yourselves.'

'We don't need no one to hold our hands,' Cato said.

'Right, then! What're you hanging around for?'

Without another word the two men turned and left. They knew exactly what was required of them and they relished the thought of what they had to do.

The rancher refilled his glass, sat in one of the soft armchairs, lit himself a large cigar and waited. He allowed his anger to simmer while he went over in his mind what he had been told. The name 'Deegan' had jolted his memory and he tried to capture the thoughts of something that had taken place in the past. At last he gave up. Perhaps the marshal would know.

Buck Clements, when he was ushered in to the big man's presence an hour and a half later, showed his displeasure at being dragged from his poker game. 'What's so hell-fired important it wouldn't wait 'til tomorrow?' he growled.

'I wouldn't need to get you here if you'd bin doing your job. Why haven't you arrested the varmints who shot down four of my men?'

The marshal tried not to sound defensive. 'If you ask me I'd say—'

'I'm not asking you. I'm telling you. By noon tomorrow I want them dead or locked up tight. One way or another they're gonna pay for what they did.'

'They've not broken no law,' the marshal offered.

'Since when did that stop you?' The rancher had given his orders and was confident that matters were going to be taken care of. His plans for owning the whole of the land he coveted could soon be concluded.

He dismissed the marshal with a wave of his hand. He was ready for his supper and he wasn't about to invite Buck Clements to his dining table.

Buck Clements was not a happy man as he rode from the ranch. Normally he enjoyed the ride, giving him time to think and to breathe the fresh air untainted by the fumes of smoke, kerosene and liquor. He had also missed much of his poker game. The meeting with the rancher and the difficult decisions he now had to make, professional and personal, had put him in a bad mood that was likely to spill over into the following day.

'Dammit,' he muttered as he spurred his horse forward.

Nevertheless, as he rode, thoughts kept coming. Lately he had settled for the easy life and, in doing so, had allowed his conscience and his ideas of right and wrong to become corrupted.

He'd persuaded himself he was doing no harm in taking money from John Gordon because the town, his town, had remained peaceful, allowing folk to live and trade freely as long as they did not enquire too deeply.

'Goddamn it!' he said again. 'I'm the law round here an' I'll do my damnedest to uphold it like I'm s'posed to.'

He told this to himself over and over again but his resolve had faded a little by the time he took his seat at the poker table where, as was customary, play would continue into the small hours of the morning.

CHAPTER 9

Billy was awakened as the dawn light entered the small window of his bedroom. He listened intently, his heart beating fast, not knowing what had disturbed his sleep. He heard nothing. But he was fully awake now and he slipped from his bed and unbolted the front door. He stood, shivering in the light wind.

Then he heard it again, a slight grating sound like a door being dragged open. He could have sworn it came from the direction of the barn. Could his pa have returned? If so, what was he doing in the barn and why would he be so silent? Then voices, whispers, a crash and a muttered oath as if someone had hurt themselves.

He was glad he hadn't lit the kerosene lamp because he now knew that whoever was out there had no right to be. Did they know he was in the house? Did they know he was alone? The thought frightened him. He was only a 13-year-old boy and sooner or later he would have to confront the men who were presently sneaking around the outbuildings. Why? He had no idea.

Perhaps they were horse thieves and he wouldn't be able to stop them.

For the space of several minutes he stood there, listening, undecided, while the faint voices continued.

'I gotta do somethin',' he told himself and the very thought stimulated him to action. He reached for the brass-framed Henry rifle his pa kept on wall pegs in the front room, found a box of .44 ammunition and loaded it. This he lay on the sill of the left-hand window. His own Yellow Boy musket he also loaded and took to the other front window, resting it carefully against the wall.

He waited. He'd used both weapons when his pa had been with him but he'd never aimed them at anybody. Target practice had been fun and his pa had been pleased with the way he'd improved.

His throat was dry. He needed a drink of water but he dared not leave his post. Except to secure the back door! He'd nearly forgotten. When he returned he saw shadowy figures emerge from the barn. Two men; he could make out their silhouettes against the lightening sky.

He watched as the men approached the house cautiously. 'Hello, the house,' one of the men called.

Making his voice as deep as he could he yelled, 'Hold it right there!'

The men froze. 'We don't mean no trouble,' one shouted. 'We come peaceful. We wanna talk, s'all.'

'Ya can say yer piece right where ya are,' Billy said.

'We wanna talk with Tom Deegan.'

'He's busy.'

'Not too busy to talk to us. We're comin' in.'

'No, you ain't!'

The Henry felt heavy in his hands as he raised the gun, firmed the butt against his shoulder as he had been taught, brought his eyes down level and steadied the barrel on the window ledge.

He controlled his breathing and squeezed the trigger.

Although he was ready for the recoil it hurt as always, but he hardly noticed the discomfort as he levered another shell into the breech. He waited to see what result the gunshot would have, his heart racing.

The first shot had gone high but it had the effect of surprise. The men who had been advancing on the cabin retreated swiftly and hunkered down behind the fence.

For the space of a long minute nothing happened. Then, 'Now, that ain't friendly. You intent on shootin' at us? Well, if that's how it is we're gonna come in whether ya like it or not.'

Billy propped the Henry against the wall, ran to the other window and picked up his Yellow Boy. He made no effort to aim.

This time the recoil sent a sharp pain up his arm but he didn't hesitate, scrambling the Henry into position once again and sending off another shot. The smell of cordite stung his nostrils.

He hoped that in this way the men would believe there was more than one person in the house and that would persuade them they'd have a fight on their hands if they wanted to continue.

'Don't be a fool, Tom Deegan,' the voice shouted.

'You remember Curly Thomson and Lofty Tate? Difficult to ferget, ain't we? Well, we're here to collect what's ours. Throw it out and we'll leave peaceful.'

Billy might have obliged if he'd known what they meant. But he had no idea. His pa had told him, 'It's best if you don't know nothin' about what I did afore you came along, Billy. Mebbe one day I'll tell ya, but fer now just trust me.' And Billy had been happy to go along with that.

He didn't let his gaze waver from the spot where the men had hidden. Movement alerted him and he sent another shot in their direction.

He drew in his breath sharply when he saw that one man was circling round with the obvious intention of attacking from the rear. He'd bolted the back door and put the shutters against the windows but he knew that wouldn't deter anyone for long. And he couldn't watch back and front at the same time.

The man out front called again. 'You've had yer chance.'

Billy sighted down the rifle, waiting for the man to move. And move he did, running, crouched, firing his pistol as he went, from left to right, making for the shelter of the small well standing in the yard no more than twenty feet away. He didn't reach it.

Billy had often fired at moving objects, and had even hit them at times. But only coyotes and rattlesnakes. This time it was different.

He gritted his teeth and took aim. He fired and the man fell. Billy gasped in shocked disbelief as he watched him go down, the echo of the gunshot sounding in his ears.

But he had no time to wonder, for the sound of splintering wood told him that the second man had gained entrance to the rear of the cabin. He didn't hesitate. He leaped out the window, carrying the musket with him, and raced to the well. With a glance across at the dead body he flung himself flat, rested the rifle on the low wall and waited.

The front door of the cabin opened and a figure appeared. It's OK, Lofty,' he shouted. 'There's no one here. Let's get this over with.'

Billy sighted and squeezed the trigger.

The man stopped in mid-stride and staggered back with blood spurting from his chest. His scream as he died sent shivers down Billy's spine. He had shot two men!

Again he heard the echo of his own shot. His hands shook, his arms felt weak and he discovered that his legs would no longer support him. He was sick. Now he began to panic. He had the chores to finish, the animals to feed and he was sure his pa would be mad with him if they hadn't been done by the time he returned.

He tried to move but his limbs failed to obey him. He lay where he was, his breathing fast and shallow, the world spinning. Screams assailed his ears. Time stopped.

Then he felt strong arms pulling him up.

'Sorry, Pa,' he mumbled. 'I ain't done the chores yet.'

'Don't you worry none about the chores,' a strange

voice told him. 'You've done well.'

He eyes snapped open and looked straight up into the face of the tall, slim stranger he had last seen in Salvation. He struggled but the grip holding him was firm.

'Lucky I come along,' the stranger said. 'You missed on all your shots.' The full meaning of that was lost on Billy as he fought to get free. He was carried into the house and sat in a chair. 'You're Billy, ain't ya?'

'Who're you?'

'Name's Slim. I'm a friend o' ya pa's.'

Billy gulped. 'No you're not! I saw ya in the street. You shot the men.'

'They was gonna shoot me.'

'You spat on them.'

'They were bad men, Billy.'

'You shouldn't've done that.'

'I also shot those two men out there in the yard,' he said. 'If I hadn't done that what d'ya reckon would've happened?'

'Dunno,' Billy mumbled, feeling some relief flood into his belly that he hadn't killed anybody. He looked up at the tall, slim man with fearful eyes. He didn't like the way he was standing so close. He didn't like the look in his eyes. He didn't like what he'd seen and heard. 'I'm obliged.'

Slim smiled. 'There, that's settled. We'll jest wait here 'til ya pa comes home. Don't mind that, do ya?' He went to the door and drew the bolt, glanced at the windows and shut them, too. 'Ya pa an' me, we're pals, see?'

Billy didn't believe him. Didn't want to believe him. He watched, awaiting his chance, because he was not intending to stay in the house with this man for longer than necessary. But already his opportunity had gone. He bit his lip as Slim unhooked a rope from the wall.

'Don't worry none,' Slim said. 'I'm not aimin' to hurt ya.' He uncoiled the rope and added, 'Unless ya pa doesn't do as he's told. Then, I s'pose I might have to kill ya.' His lips twitched in a brief smile.

Billy fought hard.

He kicked, he gouged, he used his head as a weapon and had the satisfaction of hearing Slim give a grunt of pain. He wrenched one arm free and aimed a swinging punch but managed only a glancing blow under Slim's eye.

Then it was over. He had no chance and he was soon bound securely to the chair. 'You're not a friend of my pa's,' he said, his courage returning. 'You're a killer. I seen ya an' I heard ya talkin' to the marshal.'

'Did ya, now. That's no way fer a kid to act. Not polite to listen in.' Having secured his young prisoner, Slim set about making himself at home, getting the stove going and heating up some coffee.

'Want some?'

Billy shook his head.

In spite of Mary's objections Tom and Dave Green had set off for the Triple O, but not before Mary had insisted they sit down to a good breakfast. They wore heavy coats against the chill of the morning.

'We'll catch him early,' Tom said. 'Follow my lead. If

97

what I hear about John Gordon and his henchmen is true we're walkin' into a rattler's nest an' we need to come out of it alive.'

'Yeah,' Dave agreed. 'But if'n the law can't act, or won't do anythin' about it, then I've got to.'

They slowed their horses to a walk and rode in silence, both busy with their own thoughts. Tom wondered how he had managed to get himself so involved. He had his own problems with a greedy and dangerous rancher, Lofty and Curly on the loose, Billy to worry about and a small spread to run.

Added to that was his fight with Wolf in the Hope and Pray Saloon. He was certain he hadn't heard the last of that.

At least he had an ally in the tall, slim stranger and Dave was a friend he could rely on. Also, Buck Clements might be persuaded to offer some help if needed.

And with it all he carried with him the mental picture of Alice with fire in her eyes and determination in her voice as she fearlessly faced the prospect of confronting Curly and Lofty in the saloon. He knew he'd been captivated by her beauty and impressed by her courage. He had also earned her hatred.

'Why're you doin' this for me?' Dave asked.

'Seems to me the small landowners around here have to stick together,' Tom said after some thought. 'An' I don't like to see a man swinging from the end of a rope.' Really, he thought, he had no choice. 'John Gordon's set his eyes on my land as well as yours. I reckon as how he's gettin' desperate an' his hired guns will be only too pleased to put their skills to work.'

As the sun rose they swiftly divested themselves of their coats and stopped briefly by a rill to splash water on their faces and allow their mounts to drink.

'Now we're gettin' close are ya sure you wanna continue?' Tom asked.

'Yep,' Dave replied without hesitation, fingering his Colt. 'We've come this far.'

'From here on keep yer hands clear of yer holster,' Tom warned. 'We're bein' watched.'

'Cain't see nobody.'

'From half a mile back,' Tom told him. 'Easy does it.'

The ranch house appeared as they rounded the corner of a bluff. It sat solid and permanent at the end of a small valley, an imposing, two-storey building with extensive wings on each side of the ground floor and a veranda running the full length. A stand of cotton-woods behind it set off the white-painted structure as if it had been planted there by nature.

Within a half mile of the ornate gate giving access to the enclosure they found themselves with an escort of four silent men on horseback.

'They expecting trouble?' Dave grunted.

Tom glanced from left to right. 'We're not about to give 'em any.'

They were stopped at the entrance by a cold-eyed man in black.

'Hand over yer hardware,' he said. 'Fer security reasons in case you shoot yersel's.' He grinned broadly. 'Ya walk the rest of the way.'

The two men dismounted and unbuckled their

gun-belts.

'Gotta search ya,' the man said, and ran his hands expertly over their bodies for hidden weapons, after which they were allowed to lead their horses the short distance to the hitching rail. They looped the reins and then mounted the three steps that took them up to the veranda.

The rancher was waiting for them.

As Tom and Dave stopped in front of him he held out his hand and pasted on a smile of welcome. There was no mistaking John Gordon, the wealthy owner of the Triple O ranch.

'Visitors are always welcome to the Triple O,' he boomed. His voice was cultured and imbued with the authority that comes with power and riches.

Tom turned and let his gaze travel over the hard-looking men who stood behind them in the yard. 'Don't seem so,' he said.

The rancher laughed and led them into the house. 'Take no heed o' them. They take their responsibilities very seriously. But you can never be too careful in my line of work. I have enemies.'

'I kin imagine,' Tom said, trying to inject some sarcasm into his words. Either he didn't succeed or the rancher chose to ignore him.

'With success comes envy,' John Gordon continued. 'It's as natural as carrion crows going after meat.'

Dave, who had stood silently by biting his lip, took a step forward, ignoring Tom's warning glance. 'I've heard enough o' this. Can we jest say what we've come to say and then go?'

'Certainly,' the rancher said. 'I was forgetting my manners. I won't hear of you leaving without sampling my hospitality.' He stood aside and waved them through.

'Let's discuss our business in comfort. But, first, you really must give me your opinion of this whiskey, brought in especially for me.'

There was no doubt in Tom's mind that, whatever else he might be, John Gordon was a man of money and good taste.

Tom accepted the proffered crystal glass. Dave declined with an impatient shake of his head. 'I don't drink with men who try to kill me and try to scare my family,' he grated.

The rancher ignored the outburst and waved them to comfortable armchairs.

Tom settled back, savouring the unusual flavour of the liquor. 'I kin see how a man could get used to this,' he said.

Dave, who was showing further signs of his impatience, said, 'Let's get down to it. Men in your pay left me hangin' from a tree then terrified my family. That ain't civilized. It ain't right. It's agin the law an' I'm here to give you a warning—'

'Whoa.' A deep frown replaced the smile on the rancher's face. 'I can give you my assurance that, if they did what you say, they were acting on their own. I do not condone acts of wanton violence of that nature.'

Dave smiled crookedly. 'What sort of acts of violence do you condone?'

Watching the rancher closely Tom had to admire the

101

air of innocence he was projecting as Dave continued, 'The men were in your pay.' He gestured with his thumb. 'There's more of 'em of the same kind out there. Not cowhands. Gunmen.'

The rancher showed a flicker of annoyance. 'That mebbe so,' he said. 'But while they take my money they must obey my orders and they weren't doing that.'

'They paid a high price,' Tom said.

Now there was a definite change in the older man's tone of voice. 'Seems like they did. I'm told it was you two who sent them to their graves.'

'Yeah,' Dave growled. 'An' I'll personal send to hell any more who come on the same errand.'

The rancher pulled a silk cord hanging on the wall and, almost immediately, a man knocked at the door and opened it.

'Please ask Sam Fogal to come here right away,' John Gordon said, although it was clearly an order rather than a request. As the man left the rancher turned to Tom. 'Sam's my foreman. If there's any truth in what you say, he'll know.' They waited, the rancher refilling the glasses, Dave shifting uneasily in his chair.

Sam proved to be a sharp-faced man with quick movements, dressed in jeans and check shirt. His hair hung thick and black beneath the curled brim of his Stetson.

'Sam, what's your take on the killing of Dutch and Carlos?'

Tom was studying the man and thought he saw a questioning look in his eyes before he replied, but when the answer came it came swiftly and with conviction. Either the man was telling the truth or he was quick on the uptake.

Sam showed bad teeth as he grinned. 'Damn fools took it on theirsel's to get some easy money. Got shot fer their pains.'

'That's all, Sam.' The rancher turned to Tom and Dave. 'That's what I was trying to get you to understand. What possible reason could I have to send men out to your farm?'

'For the reason you've bin after my land fer long enough.'

The rancher raised his hands as if giving in to the argument. 'It's true your piece of ground would be useful to me. I've offered you a fair price.'

'Which I've rejected before and do so now. You've offered nothing like what the place is worth. I'm not selling and I'll be damned if any critter's gonna drive me off.'

The big man indicated that the meeting was over.

Tom rose and placed his empty glass on the side table. As they made their way to the door the rancher said, 'I suggest it may be in your own best interests to accept.'

Dave whirled. 'What in tarnation d'ya mean by that?'

'Nothing sinister, I assure you. Only that I know how hard it is for you homesteaders to make a living.'

Tom had had the opportunity of assessing the rancher face to face and he now had little doubt that the man's reputation for charm and ruthlessness was well deserved. 'Do we have your word you'll rein in ya men?' he asked. 'Mebbe they're actin' on their own, mebbe not. Either way this has gotta stop.'

103

'And I need your word there'll be no more rustling of my cattle.'

'Damn you,' Dave shouted. 'You know they were planted.'

'You've outstayed yer welcome,' the rancher said abruptly.

As they walked down the steps into the yard he stood in the doorway, watching them go with a cold stare. They were met by one of the hard men holding their horses ready. He handed them their guns and cartridge belts. The only trouble was that all the cartridges had been removed.

'What's the meaning of this?' Tom demanded.

The man shrugged. 'I told ya. Security.'

'Whose security might that be?'

'Don't really matter,' he was told. 'That's how it's gonna be.'

They strapped on their empty belts and mounted up. There was nothing to be gained by arguing. Their progress to the ornate gateway giving exit onto the trail was watched by more men of the same type; gunmen for sure.

Tom leaned across to Dave. 'I don't b'lieve these *hombres* mean us to get out of here alive.'

'What're we gonna do about it?' Dave asked.

'Not sure yet,' Tom said. 'Keep yer eyes open.'

CHAPTER 10

Billy met Slim's hard eyes as the tall man stared down at his captive. He had seen the man in action and had no doubt of what he was capable of doing. But he still wondered what it was all about.

'These ropes're hurting,' he said, needing to break the silence.

'I'd like to undo them, really I would,' Slim grinned. 'But you're a tough young man an' I don't wanna have to wrestle you agin.'

'You'd best go afore Pa gets back.'

Slim shrugged and took the makings from his pocket. 'Think yer pa's got any cigars stashed away?'

'I wouldn't tell you even if he had,' Billy said.

'P'raps he's got some liquor, then.'

'Wouldn't know about that.'

'Ah, well.' Slim struck a Vesta on his pants. 'This'll have to do meantime.'

Billy shifted uncomfortably in his bonds. 'How long are you gonna keep me here?'

'All depends. We kin prob'ly keep ourselves amused

somehow. First things first, though.' He took a swig of coffee and faced Billy. 'I'm gonna ask you agin, where is the money yer pa took from the robbery?'

'Pa hasn't robbed nobody.' He had no idea what the man was talking about.

'Yer pa was an outlaw, Billy.'

'Don't believe you.'

Slim rubbed his chin. 'I wonder if yer tellin' the truth.'

'What's there to lie about?'

'Our two friends lying in the dirt outside reckoned they were close. They made a good job o' searching the buildings out there an' couldn't find what they were lookin' fer. That leaves this cabin an' I guess there ain't many hiding places in here fer a bag full o' dollars.'

Billy's mouth sprang open. 'D'ya think if Pa had a stash of money he'd be working as hard as he does just to make a living?'

Slim grunted. 'Seems to me ya don't know much so we're gonna find out what ya do know. Thirteen years ago yer pa was part of a gang that held up the stage travellin' to Salvation an' carryin' a sizeable tin box full o' money fer the bank there. The money was fer the local rancher, John Gordon, who was intendin' to use it to expand his spread by hiring guns. Not the rancher nor the bank nor Wells Fargo were too pleased when it was stole.'

'What's that gotta do with us?'

'Patience, boy! Did yer pa not teach you some manners? The gang was led by yer pa's uncle, the preacher. Yer pa was a member of that gang. The

106

robbery went wrong. People got shot an' the coach caught fire. Yer pa found a very young boy still alive in the coach.' He paused, watching Billy closely. 'Yer pa was a hero. That boy was you.'

'Ya talkin' nonsense!'

'How old are ya?'

'Coming up fourteen.'

'Fits then, don't it?'

Billy writhed but only managed to inflict pain on himself. 'You're tellin' lies. Did yer pa not tell ya it was bad—'

He stopped speaking as Slim hit him hard across the face.

Slim went on, 'Yer pa took the boy an' the money an' was s'posed to stash it in a special place. But he didn't, an' those two out there, they came lookin' for it when they came outa prison.' He pointed to the yard. 'One o' them nice men, afore he died, was kind enough to tell me this an' more. I believe him on account he was kinda in pain at the time an' it was hurtin' him somethin' terrible.'

'I don't know nothin' about that,' Billy said. 'I told ya we ain't got no money. Let me go an' I'll even help you search.' His mind was struggling to take in what Slim was telling him.

'I'm obliged but I'll not be acceptin' yer offer. I b'lieve the money was never found.' He stared at Billy. 'If it ain't here yer pa knows where it's hid. One way or another he'll tell me. He ain't really yer pa but I don't s'pose he'd want to see ya hurt. Either of ya.'

'He'll kill ya.'

'Don't doubt it. That is, if he gets the chance. He'll be here soon.' A smile spread across Slim's face. 'Though he might be a while yet. Last time I saw him he was goin' off with a good-looking young lady. Gives me time to clear up outside an' search the place.'

As he was talking he took out his knife and felt the edge of the blade with his thumb. He stood and crossed to stand behind the boy. He stroked his hair, then caressed his neck. He let Billy feel the coldness of the steel on his skin. Billy shuddered.

This seemed to amuse him. 'I don't make a habit o' hurting young boys, but it won't come to that, I'm sure.'

'You . . . you're a snake!' Billy hissed.

'I've bin called worse,' Slim smiled. 'Now, I'm sorry but it's time to shut you up an' wait. Don't want yer pa to know we're here, do we?'

Billy could do nothing to stop him as he bound a gag over his mouth. 'Sorry to do this to ya,' Slim said again. 'But I doubt it'll be fer long an' you might feel the urge to shout out at the wrong time.'

Now Billy felt the panic rising in his chest and he couldn't control it as Slim tied a blindfold over his eyes. He sucked air in through the gag. Then he was lifted up, chair and all, and carried through to what he could tell from the change in sound to be the back bedroom.

His bonds were tight; he could neither see nor speak but he held on to the thought that his pa would save him. He heard the door shut and he was alone.

Tom and Dave were clear of the gate to the Triple O as they headed back. There had been no sign of trouble.

'Stay alert,' Tom said, as he adjusted the crown of his Stetson. 'At the first sign we ride as fast as we can.' He took out his Colt, span the chamber and examined it. After a moment he slipped it back in its holster. 'We jus' may have an ace up our sleeves yet. Depends what they have in mind.'

'Mebbe they don't mean us no harm,' Dave said, hopefully. 'Jus' trying to put a scare in us.'

'Don't count on it.'

They had travelled at an easy pace for a mile, conserving the energy of their mounts, and had reached a point where the trail narrowed between two rock faces. Without warning a horseman appeared from the cover of an outcrop. In his hand he held a pistol. A second, younger man followed. His hands were empty but one was held close to his holster.

'Where do ya think ya going?' the older man growled. They reined in.

'We're leaving. What's it to you?'

'Git down from yer horses.'

Dave looked at Tom, who nodded and slid from the saddle. 'Now what?'

'I'm gonna kill ya.'

'We're unarmed.'

'Don't look that way to me.' His gun didn't waver.

'Our guns're empty.'

'I reckon that's bad luck. Mine's full. Three slugs apiece oughta do it.' His face split into a grin as his finger tightened on the trigger.

Tom held up his hands. 'Wait. Sure, you're hell-bent on killin' us an' we can't do nothin' about that. But, before you do, I'd be mighty obliged if you'd settle a bet. I wouldn't want to die not knowing.'

The gunman hesitated. Doubt crept into his eyes. 'What sorta bet?'

Tom indicated Dave. 'This man claims I'm the fastest draw he's ever seen. He reckons I kin outdraw anyone.'

'So what?'

'You look as if yer no mean shooter yerself. D'ya reckon you could outdraw me?'

The gunman guffawed as he glanced at his partner. 'What d'ya think, Cato? Shall we show him afore he bites the dust?' Receiving a nod of approval, he replaced his Colt in its holster and slipped from the saddle. 'Who's gonna be the judge?'

'Cato if he's of a mind,' Tom suggested. 'An' mebbe Dave here. Make yer move when yer ready.'

The two men faced each other, legs spread. Their hands flashed down and the two guns appeared as if by magic. They waited for the verdict. It was a split decision and pride demanded they try again. Too close to call.

'Last time,' the gunman said. 'I'm tired o' this game. This time I'm gonna pull the trigger.' He replaced his Colt. 'Say yer prayers.'

Tom kept his levelled. 'Shuck yer gun-belts,' he snarled.

Neither of the men moved. 'Ya gonna shoot us with an empty gun?'

Tom squeezed the trigger and a fountain of dust sprang up at Seth's feet. The horses shied.

'Where did ya git—'

'I said get rid o' yer hardware!' Tom's voice took on an edge that was not lost on the gunmen. 'I don't wanna tell ya again.'

The men hesitated, but only for a moment. It could have gone either way but common sense prevailed. They had seen the speed at which Tom could draw and reckoned he could shoot with the same skill. Their gun-belts fell into the dirt. 'I don't wanna kill ya,' Tom said. 'So start walking.' He pointed in the direction of the ranch.

'You'll pay fer this,' Seth snarled. 'There ain't no place ya kin hide. Best start sayin' yer prayers right now.'

'If I want yer advice I'll ask fer it,' Tom said and smiled as he watched Cato step reluctantly from his horse and then the two of them trudge uncomfortably back down the rocky trail in their riding boots.

'I reckon they'll be feelin' the heat by the time they get back to the ranch. Help yerself to ammunition,' he told Dave. 'Then we'll heave their hardware down the side of some ravine.'

They filled their guns and belts and mounted up. 'Best git going afore they cotton on to what's happened.' Tom slapped the riderless horses on their rumps and sent them careering away. 'They'll find their own way back soon enough.'

They rode fast, making for Salvation where they hoped they might enlist the help of the marshal, Buck Clements being the only law available. Glancing behind on their back trail Tom was relieved to see no immediate signs of pursuit.

111

As they eased their pace Dave said, 'Where in tarnation did yer get the slugs?'

Tom grinned. 'I alus keep one in my hat fer luck. It was a habit my uncle got me into.'

'He wasn't all bad, then.'

'I learned a lot from him,' Tom admitted.

Dave considered this. 'Sure paid off. But you said you kept one slug. You must've had more'n that.'

'Nope,' Tom said. 'Only one.'

Dave grinned. 'You mean yer gun was empty after you fired that shot in the dirt?'

'Yep.'

'Playin' with fire, weren't ya?'

Tom shrugged 'Sure I was, but I couldn't think of a better idea on the spur of the moment. It worked, didn't it?'

Dave couldn't deny that.

They took the trail to Salvation, intending to talk to the marshal.

CHAPTER 11

As soon as they entered the town Tom and Dave made for the law office. The marshal was sitting back on the small porch, feet up on the rail, Stetson pulled low, eyes closed. There was little doubt that he was asleep.

'Seems a pity to wake him,' Dave said.

They reined in, dismounted and looped the reins over the hitch rail, not concerned with how much noise they made. Buck Clements slowly opened his eyes and let his feet drop, pushed back his hat and leaned forward, a scowl of annoyance on his face.

'You bringin' me more trouble?' he growled.

'Depends what ya call trouble.' Tom said.

'I was gonna come lookin' fer you two, anyway,' the marshal drawled. 'Need to talk.'

'That's what we've come fer,' Tom said.

'Well, that's cosy. We're all of a mind, ain't we?' He waved them into the office, followed them and shut the door. 'Siddown!'

His change of tone came as a shock but they did as he said. When they looked up they found that the lawman had drawn his Colt and was levelling it at them. As he lowered himself into his old desk chair his gun didn't waver.

'I'm indebted to ya for paying me a visit,' he grinned. 'Saved me a load o' trouble come lookin' fer ya. Now, afore we chat, I'll ask ya to take out yer weapons, real easy, and lay 'em on the desk.'

'What in tarnation for?' Tom bellowed. 'You arrestin' us?'

'No one kin say ya not quick on the uptake,' the marshal said with a shake of his head. 'Yer goddamn right I'm arrestin' ya. Both.'

The two men glared at him but reluctantly placed their pistols on the desk. 'Why're ya doin' this?' Tom asked. 'We ain't broke no law.'

'Wouldn't be too sure about that,' the lawman grated. 'Rustlin' beef an' murder are crimes in my book.'

'Can't disagree with that,' Tom said, waiting for the marshal's attention to wander. 'But yer arrestin' the wrong men. Rustlin' an' murder ain't what we're about.'

The lawman took a firmer grip on his gun. 'I've bin marshal here fer nigh-on ten years. Deputy afore that. I've seen men like you come and go. Men who reck-oned they was above the law. Most met their Maker at the end of a gun. Seen a few of 'em off myself. Whatever you think, I do what I reckon is right.'

Dave shifted in his chair. 'I've seen no evidence of that.'

'That's the trouble wi' you farmers. Only look to the

law when it suits ya. But I'm tellin' ya here an' now when ya step over the line I'm here to put a stop to it. Any quarrel wi' that?'

'None at all,' Tom said. 'Only trouble is we ain't broken no law.'

'Jury might have other ideas 'bout that.'

'If it gets that far,' Dave said. 'They tried to kill us out at the ranch.'

The marshal scratched his head. 'So ya say.'

'We're lookin' fer justice,' Tom told him, feeling his anger rise. 'Or is it that you've got yer orders from someone who wants us dead?'

The marshal eased himself in his chair. 'Best tell me your side o' the story.'

They told him and he listened without comment. Tom was halfway to revising his opinion of Buck Clements. Perhaps the man really was trying to be fair. Or was he trying to please two masters at the same time – the law and the big rancher? If he was he trod a fine line.

When they had finished the lawman scratched his head even harder as if he found it difficult to reach a decision. Then he surprised them both. 'I'm gonna let you spend a night in jail while I have a talk with John Gordon. Dependin' on that I'll be able to decide yer future. Seems more'n likely I'll be savin' ya lives as well.'

'How d'ya make that out?'

'You've made a fistful o' enemies in a very short time an' somethin' tells me you haven't made things any better in the last few hours.'

Tom looked at Dave and raised his eyebrows. 'You're

very well informed.'

Buck Clements smirked. 'That's what I'm paid fer. And to keep gunplay off the streets.'

'We ain't looking fer gunplay, Marshal. Fact is we're trying to avoid it. That's why we've come to you.'

'That's mighty sensible of ya.'

'If you're really concerned about us,' Tom said. 'You'd let us take care of ourselves.'

'Seein' dead bodies don't agree with me.'

'So why not be friendly and let us go?'

'Like I said, I'm paid to uphold the law and, until I'm satisfied you haven't broken any, I'm keepin' you here.'

Tom shrugged. 'Guess you'll be needin' our gunbelts, then.' With a slight shake of his head at Dave he shoved back his chair and unbuckled his belt, sensing Dave's surprise as he did so. He grasped both ends in one hand and made to lay it on the desk next to the guns.

Instead, hard and swift, he swept the belt from left to right, sweeping papers and the Colts to the floor and, at the same time, knocking the marshal's weapon sideways.

'Goddamn it!' the marshal yelled, letting go of his gun as the belt bit into his knuckles, but managing to grab it up again with his other hand.

The slight delay gave Tom his chance. He dived for the door. There was no sense in attempting to pick up one of the guns because they had slipped across the floor into the far corner away from the door. From the corner of his eye he saw the marshal's gun barrel swing his way.

He threw himself at the door, wrenched it open and slipped through as the marshal's gun roared and a slug smacked into the woodwork, missing him by a good three feet. He staggered out onto the boardwalk, twisted, rolled and regained his feet, expecting a bullet to follow.

But for some reason the marshal had not followed him out. Neither had Dave Green. There was no way he could go back for the farmer. Already folk were staring warily at him, not quite sure what was going on. He smiled at them and tried to appear casual.

He realized with some surprise that he was still holding his cartridge belt and he quickly buckled it round his hips. It was useless, however, without a gun and, as he strode away, he set his mind to thinking how he could obtain one, for he was sure he would need it before much longer.

He made his way cautiously to his aunt's store, trying not to draw attention to himself and peering behind him in case the marshal took it into his head to follow. There was also the threat of hired guns from the ranch who might be looking for him. At the store he would find Billy and, with any luck, there would be a gun he could borrow, remembering that Billy's own rifle had been left back at the farm.

He felt far from relaxed as he pushed open the door. Jane was behind the counter coping with the influx of customers. He glanced at the clock on the wall, surprised to find it was past midday. So much had happened in a few hours.

'Where's Billy?' he asked as soon as Jane was free.

117

His aunt looked at him in surprise, then concern. 'I thought he was with you.'

A hollow feeling developed in Tom's stomach. Surely nothing else could go wrong. 'I left him with you.'

'He rode off just after I'd closed up. A boy came to the house, said Billy was going home to you. It was too late to stop him. I told you he was a—'

Tom's stomach churned. 'I haven't bin home.'

'Well, where could he have gone?'

'How the hell should I know? I left him in your care.' He was angry with his aunt but bit back on his frustration. 'If he rode home, then he'll be there now, waiting on me. Did he say why he was going?'

'No, except earlier he'd told me he thought you were in danger and he wanted to warn you about it.'

'What danger might that've bin?'

Jane sounded contrite. 'Tom, I really don't know. It was just after he'd seen two men shot down in the street.'

'Who did the shooting?'

'One man, tall and slim. Dangerous-looking. You could ask the marshal. He could tell you.'

Tom ran his hands through his hair. 'Cain't do that. I'll explain later.' He couldn't risk going back.

'Right now I need two things from you: a gun and a horse.' His own grey was standing outside the law office. 'Can you oblige?'

'Where are yours?' She didn't wait for an answer. 'I can let you have my husband's old Colt,' she said. 'He always kept it handy in case he needed it. Never had cause, though.' She rummaged through a drawer below

the counter and came up with a Colt .45 with a 5½"
barrel. 'Here it is. Hasn't bin used for years.'

He took the gun from her and examined it, finding it
in good condition but empty. He blew the dust off, span
and tested the mechanism. 'Seems OK. I'm obliged.' He
filled all six chambers from his gun-belt and slid the
weapon into his holster. Only then did he realize how
naked he had felt without it. 'Dunno how to thank you.'

He peered out the front door, looking up the street
towards the law office where his horse was still tethered.
There was no hope of retrieving it.

As he watched, Buck Clements stepped out, stood for
a while, went back in and shut the door. Tom suspected
that Dave would by now be locked in his cell.

'Any chance of a horse?'

Jane nodded. 'A sweet little sorrel in the stable back
at the house. You'll find a saddle and harness there.'

He opened the rear door, which backed on to an
alley and carefully allowed his eyes to become adjusted.
He did not expect trouble at this point.

'Just take care of yourself,' Jane called.

That was his intention. 'I aim to. Thanks fer everything.'

Once outside he remained still for a full minute then
made his way through the back lots to his aunt's house.

There he soon found everything as she had
promised. He spoke gently to the sorrel while she
patiently allowed him to saddle her and tighten the
cinch.

In the small cooking area of the house there was a
canteen, which he filled with water. He put some

biscuits in his pocket, mounted and set off on the trail for home.

He felt easier now that he was armed and had a horse beneath him.

He met no trouble and pushed the sorrel hard as soon as they had cleared the town boundary. The horse responded well and seemed to enjoy the pace he was asking of her. He could only pray that Billy was safe.

He cautiously approached his cabin, slowing the mare as he reached the top of a knoll from where he had a good view of the building and surrounding area.

It all seemed peaceful with smoke rising slowly into the still air, chickens pecking in the yard at the back, the horses quiet in the corral, Billy's among them. Nothing wrong there, so what was causing his concern?

Everything was too quiet. There were no signs of activity.

Tom frowned. It would be unlike Billy not to be working at something. He remained motionless and let the mare crop the succulent grass. Eventually, seeing nothing to justify his caution, he set the sorrel down the slope and entered the yard. Perhaps, he reasoned, Billy was out tending the cows. No, that couldn't be. Not without his horse.

Then where the hell was he?

Tom slid from the saddle and tethered the mare, then started towards the door of the cabin. A sixth sense warned him that something was wrong; his hand hovered by his gun butt. He stopped.

As he started forward again the cabin door opened. He expected to see his son but instead Slim stood there leaning easily against the doorpost, hands hanging loose by his side.

Tom's surprise gave way to recognition. 'Slim! S'prised to see ya but yer more'n welcome. Seen anything of my son, Billy?'

'Yeah,' Slim drawled. 'Had us a long chat. Good, strong boy ya got there. Must be proud o' him.'

Tom relaxed. 'Yep, I'm real proud of him. Know where he is now?'

'Sure. I've jus' made some coffee. Looks like you could use some.'

'Guess so. But I have to see—'

Suddenly he was aware of Slim's gun pointing at his chest. 'What the hell! And what's the idea of the gun?' His impulse was to go for his own weapon but he had hesitated too long.

'I wouldn't do that!' Slim's .45 moved threateningly. He pasted on an easy smile.

'Who are ya?'

'Name's Slim. Least that's what folk call me.'

'I know ya name,' Tom grated. 'But who are ya? What ya doin' here?'

'Now, if ya just unbuckle yer belt an' let it fall I'll be able to answer all yer questions. And, of course, you can tell me everything I want to know.'

'Where's Billy?'

A harshness crept into Slim's manner. 'Shuck yer gun. Then we can talk.'

'Where's my son?' He undid his belt.

'Drop it! Now kick it away.'

Tom saw no point in doing otherwise. He shrugged.

121

'I asked ya about my son.'

'Billy's OK. Let's keep it that way. He was kind enough to let me in.'

'I wanna see him.'

'All in good time.'

Tom eyed the man, a few inches taller but far less muscular than he was and he reckoned that, given the opportunity, he could easily overpower him. At that moment, however, Slim appeared to be holding all the aces.

Slim ushered him inside where they stood facing each other. Tom heard a sound from the back room and knew immediately what it was. Ignoring Slim he strode to the door and thrust it open.

He whirled on Slim. 'If yer've harmed him you're a dead man.' He rushed over and gently removed the blindfold and gag from his son's face. 'Has he hurt ya, son?'

Billy's eyes lit up and he smiled bravely. He dragged in air and moistened his dry lips, spitting out small pieces of cloth. He shook his head.

'I'm OK, Pa.'

Tom took a step towards Slim. 'Why've ya done this? He's only a boy.'

Slim chuckled, a sound that had no humour in it. 'I was forced to tie him up. He's strong fer his age.' He pointed to the injuries on his own face. 'Reckon he did more damage than I did.'

Tom started to loosen the ropes but Slim waved him away with the barrel of his gun. 'There's a small matter outstandin', in case it's slipped ya memory. You're gonna tell me where the money is an' we kin all go home.'

'Why bring the boy into this? He knows nothing about it.'

'I already reckoned on that but he's my insurance. It's very simple. You tell me where you stashed the money an' I let the boy go. If ya don't, well, it's plain enough, ain't it?'

Tom looked over at his son. 'Stick with it, Billy. This coyote ain't gonna kill neither of us.'

Slim chortled. 'An' what makes ya think that?'

'Because,' Tom said slowly, 'I'm gonna kill you.'

'Well, that's settled then, ain't it? Dunno how ya reckon on doing it, though. Now, I'm not a patient man. Where's the money?' His pistol turned menacingly towards Billy.

Tom took the chance and hurled himself at the man but Slim was ready for him and brought the barrel round in a vicious arc to connect with Tom's head. He sank to the floor.

'Pa!' Billy yelled and strained against the ropes binding him.

Slim took a step back. 'There was no need fer that,' he drawled and waited for Tom to recover. 'Now, let's go back into the other room and talk.'

Tom staggered to his feet and Slim pushed him roughly through the doorway, following closely behind. 'Now, siddown an' start talking.'

When Tom remained silent Slim raised his voice so that Billy could hear. 'Billy, tell yer pa what I'm gonna do to you if he doesn't co-operate.'

'Tell him yerself!' Billy yelled.

Slim rubbed his chin. 'Well, I don't need to spell it out, do I?'

'I buried the money,' Tom said through gritted teeth.

'That's what I reckoned. Where?'

'In town.'

'I told ya I'm not a patient man. Where did ya bury it?'

Tom's head was clearing. 'It was over thirteen years ago. I was just a kid. I'd seen men killed. I was in a panic an' I wanted to get rid of it quicker than a man kin spit.'

'I'm waiting.'

'What I'm saying,' Tom said, hoping he was sounding sincere, 'is that I can't recall exactly. Somewhere at the east end of Main Street. Of course,' he added, 'the town's grown since then an' it may be there's bin something built on top of it by now.'

Slim seemed to consider this. 'If you're playing games I'll kill ya son first an' then you.'

'I'm sure I can take ya to it,' Tom said.

Slim nodded. 'Right. Let's say I b'lieve ya – fer now. We're goin' outside an' you'll saddle up horses fer me an' Billy. An' don't get any more ideas about jumping me. I've taken prisoners more dangerous than you. I won't kill ya yet but you'll hurt some.'

Under Slim's direction Tom saddled up the two mounts and they started back for the cabin. Before they reached the door the bark of Slim's Colt broke the silence and Tom was flung around as a slug bit into his right arm. A split second later he felt the pain where his flesh had been torn and blood began to flow.

He whirled. 'What in tarnation!'

Slim grinned. 'A precaution,' he said. 'We're gonna ride into town, all three of us, an' I don't trust you not to try something. Don't worry. The slug didn't strike bone, 'less I'm losin' my touch.'

Holding his arm, Tom entered the house and searched for something to stem the blood. He tore up a sheet, used some as a pad and the rest as an improvised sling. He glared at Slim. 'I'm definitely gonna kill ya fer that.' He dressed his wound as best he could. 'What now?'

'We wait,' Slim said.

'Fer what?'

'Fer the sun to go down.'

'In that case I'm gonna untie my son an' we're gonna have us somethin' to eat.'

Slim nodded. 'OK by me. Could do with some home cookin'. But,' he snarled, 'if either of you think o' pulling somethin' fancy, I've got the answer here.' He stroked the butt of his Colt. 'And I won't shoot to kill.'

CHAPTER 12

Alice and her ma had waited anxiously for the return of Tom and Dave. The Triple O ranch was no more than a two-hour ride away and the men had said they would be straight back after talking to the rancher.

They had now been gone for most of the day and there was still no sign of them. 'What d'you think could've happened?' Alice voiced their thoughts. 'If they've got into trouble we're the only ones who knew where they were going.'

'Your pa's capable of taking care of himself,' her ma suggested, seemingly in an effort to comfort herself rather than from conviction. 'And Tom seems more than capable.'

'I don't like it,' Alice said. 'I'm not going to wait here any longer. I think we should both ride into town and speak to the marshal. He'll surely know what to do.'

Her ma finished the work she was doing. 'If you feel that way you'd best go. I'll wait here. They won't want to find an empty house when they return.'

Alice nodded. 'Sure you'll be all right here on your own?'

'D'you really think I've never been in the house on my own? Joe's due back inside of two hours. If you haven't returned by sundown I'll ask him to sleep in the house. Of course I'll be all right. If the men have gone into Salvation instead of coming back here I'll be as mad as hell.'

Alice, who had never heard her ma speak in such a way, smiled wryly and set about preparing herself for the journey. She was concerned about leaving her ma alone and anxious about the fate of her pa.

Over and above that, although she found it difficult to admit it to herself, she was worried for Tom. She wanted to hate him and told herself that she did. But she knew that was a lie.

'If it's too late to start back I'll stay with Shelley,' she said.

She waited another hour then set off. Nearly an hour after that she reined in outside the marshal's office, slipped from the saddle, mounted the three steps and knocked on the door. She entered without waiting for a reply.

Buck Clements was seated at his desk, shuffling papers from one side to the other. He stood when he saw who his visitor was.

'I think I need your help,' Alice said without preamble.

The marshal sat down and took the makings from his pocket. There was a smile on his face as he eased back in the chair, struck a Vesta and applied the flame.

127

'You've come to the right place,' he said, drawing the smoke into his lungs. 'What can I do fer you?'

His smile angered Alice and she wondered if indeed she had come to the right place. Was the marshal treating her visit as a big joke?

'I'm not sure,' she began. 'My pa and Tom Deegan rode out this morning to talk to John Gordon, the rancher at the Triple O. They should've been back some hours ago.'

'Ah, Tom Deegan,' the lawman mused and held out his hand for Alice to see. 'He did this to me afore he rushed outa my office earlier today. I owe him one fer that.'

Alice opened her eyes wide. 'Why would he do that? Tom Deegan gave us help when we needed it,' she said with more emotion than she intended. 'That's more than you have ever done.'

'Stop. We've got off on the wrong foot. I guess you've come to see yer pa.'

'I'm looking to you to find out what might have happened to him. Maybe you could take a ride out to the ranch.'

Buck Clements's smile became broader. 'No need fer that.' He raised his voice and turned his head towards the cells. 'Dave! Yer daughter's here to see ya.'

Alice leaped to her feet. 'You've locked him up in—' She stopped as her pa walked in through the heavy dividing door. 'Pa! What're you doing here?' She flung herself into his arms. 'I thought you were. . . .'

The marshal indicated that they should both sit down. 'I'll explain if you'll jus' listen,' he said. 'If ya'd bin here earlier you'd've seen their hosses outside but I had them taken down to the livery. Didn't wanna advertise that I had guests. It was my intention to keep yer pa and Tom Deegan safe in the jail. Not locked up, ya unnerstand. But Deegan had other ideas. He left in a hurry an' I wasn't about to go running after him.'

Alice tried to absorb this. 'Safe? Why shouldn't they be safe?'

'Both yer pa and Deegan seem to have upset the rancher and some of his hired guns. There're at least two *hombres* in town looking fer blood, an' it's not their own they're after.

'I don't want trouble in my town an' I reckoned that the best way of avoidin' it was to keep the two sides apart until they all cooled down.'

'Where's Tom Deegan now?' Alice asked.

'Far as I'm informed he lit out fer home. I b'lieve his son went there in a hurry last night. There's nothing I can do about that.'

Dave placed his hand on Alice's shoulder. 'What the marshal says makes sense. When those men've filled theirsel's with liquor and find they've got nobody to fight they'll go back to the ranch an' we can go home.'

Alice gazed intently at the marshal, assessing his motives. 'Are you going to keep me here, too?'

The lawman returned her stare. 'Neither of you are my prisoners,' he said. 'You can do what you think best. But, afore you make up ya minds I'd like to tell you a few facts. Facts about Tom Deegan and the stage hold-up thirteen years ago that might interest you.'

'Why would it be of any interest to me?' Alice asked.

Buck Clements smiled. 'Dunno, but if ya don't wanna listen then ya free to go now.'

Alice stayed seated. 'Go on.'

'OK. Now, don't interrupt. I recall the hold-up very well,' he began. 'I was a deputy here at the time so I wasn't involved in the investigation an' I wasn't part of the posse that set out to chase the varmints. But it made big news throughout the territory.

'It was later that I learned some of the facts. Seems there were only four outlaws, that is if you don't count the young boy who had been taken along by his uncle, the preacher, Morgan Jones – the goddamn varmint.

'Excuse the language, Alice, but if there's any justice he's ended up in hell, because he got a couple o' slugs in the shoot-out an' that killed him before the law could catch up with him.'

Alice nodded, her face screwed up at the memory. 'I know the boy was Tom Deegan. He told me. I hate him for what he did. My own brother was shot dead at that time.'

'As far as we know Tom Deegan took no part in the killin's. Fact is, I'm sure he didn't want to be there. But he was an' he watched it happen without bein' able to do anythin' to stop it.

'What he did do was pull a young child out of the flames. It was a boy, under a year old. With its parents dead we made a search to find relations who'd be willing to take him in. No one was traced so the alternative was to put the boy in an orphanage.

'Tom Deegan wasn't gonna have that. It didn't happen to him when his parents died of the fever so he didn't want it to happen to the child. With the help of his aunt he brought the boy up himself.' He paused. 'You've already met Billy, I believe.'

'How do you know all this?' Dave asked as his daughter remained silent.

'I made some enquiries of my own. Feelings ran high jus' after the murders an' Tom Deegan would've bin put on trial if folk had known he'd bin part of the gang. He'd've ended up in prison with the other two outlaws an' I didn't think that was right.'

Alice smiled for the first time. 'Thanks, Marshal. I'm glad you told us. But what happened to the money?'

'That I can't answer,' the lawman said. 'It would've done my reputation good if I could've found it. With six people dead the outlaws left, taking it with them. They stashed it some place, no one knows where, an' they weren't talking.'

Seth and Cato had left the Triple O ranch for Salvation eagerly anticipating their mission. They had full confidence in their own prowess with a six-shooter and took pride and joy in killing.

Now, having failed to find the men they were gunning for, they had settled themselves in the Hope and Pray Saloon, indulging their appetites for whiskey. 'I'm gonna have a look round,' Seth told his pard after some hours had passed. 'Ain't no sense comin' all this way fer nothin', is there?'

Cato drained his glass. 'An' we ain't goin' back to tell the boss we failed. Those two coyotes've gotta be somewhere.'

'When we find 'em we'll have us some fun,' Seth said. 'Won't have no trouble from the marshal. Boss told him to keep outa the way.'

They pushed their way through the batwings and, by habit, split up immediately, Seth crossing over the main street to take up position on the boardwalk on the other side.

They swaggered, shoving others aside. They were not seeking popularity and treated the town and its inhabitants as their property. And no one dared challenge them. They walked the length of the street but, in spite of asking questions of the folk they met, there was no sign of their quarry.

Cato, who had worked up another thirst, signalled to Seth that they should make their way back to the saloon for refreshments. Seth readily agreed. They would resume their search later.

It was much later when Cato had won a considerable amount at the tables. Seth helped him scoop up his winnings and hauled him to his feet, an action that did not please the cowpokes who had lost their money.

'This ain't right,' said one. 'Things was jus' startin' to change.' He half rose but he found Seth's gun pointing at his chest.

'Wanna make somethin' of it?' Seth growled.

'Things ain't right,' the man said.

'You'd best make yerself clear.' Seth's gun didn't waver.

The cowpoke shrugged. 'I'm only sayin' that we should be given the chance to get some of our money back.'

'Well, now you've said it. But it ain't your money to git back. It's Cato's an' he won it fair an' square. Unless yer think otherwise.' Not receiving an answer he grabbed Cato's arm and dragged him outside. 'We gotta job to do,' he grated. 'Have ya forgot that?'

'I ain't forgot,' Cato snarled. 'Bin lookin' forward to it.'

'Right, let's git to it.'

CHAPTER 13

The sun was dropping towards the horizon as Slim roped Billy's horse to his own and secured the boy's hands to the pommel.

Tom rode ahead, his mind working hard on how to turn the tables on the bounty hunter, as he led the way along the trail to Salvation. He knew that Slim would have no hesitation in carrying out his threat to hurt Billy if he thought it necessary. He did not want to give him cause. He couldn't risk any harm coming to his son.

Moreover, his injured arm would prevent him from using a gun with any accuracy even if he could get hold of one. That had obviously been Slim's intention in shooting him and he had to admit it was very effective.

He turned and looked over his shoulder. 'I need to ride next to my son.'

'No deal,' Slim said.

'I'm OK, Pa.' The boy sat upright on the bay, clearly wanting to show his pa that he was not afraid.

'Everything's gonna be all right, Billy,' Tom said.

'This rattlesnake ain't gonna see daylight tomorrow.'

Slim guffawed. 'Like yer spirit. I'm not only gonna see the dawn but I'm gonna ride away a very rich man. All you have to do is show me where you buried the money. Now look ahead an' shuddup.'

Despite his confident words Tom had no idea what he was going to do, with very few options left to him. He could hand the money over to Slim and hope that would be the end of the matter.

Or he could try to fool the man and wait for his chance. But his assessment was that Slim would not be easily fooled and, having taken that option, there would be no going back.

He guessed he couldn't rely on help from the good folk of Salvation nor an intervention by the marshal, who, earlier on that day, had wanted to lock him up.

Slim had delayed their departure so that night would cover their activities. The shadows were deepening as they neared the town and Tom made for the east end of Main Street. The bell tower of the church at the other end gleamed pink as it caught the rays of the dying sun.

He reined in and waited for Slim and Billy to draw alongside. 'It's somewhere around here,' he said.

'You'll have to do better'n that,' Slim growled.

'I told ya, it was a long time ago and there've bin new buildings here since then.'

Tom made a pretence of studying the area. 'There was a tree standing hereabouts,' he said. 'Must've bin cut down.'

'I'm givin' ya one minute to come up with an answer,' Slim snarled. 'Then I'm gonna. . . .' He made

135

a move towards Billy.

'All right. I remember somethin' now. There was an old well, partly filled in. I put it in there.'

'That's better.' Slim grinned. 'Knew it'd come to ya. Where is this well?'

'Yeah.' Tom pointed. 'Over there.' He guided his horse past the livery and stopped at a gap between buildings. 'Here it is. Couldn't be built on, I guess.'

'Lucky fer you,' Slim said. 'Git digging.'

Tom dismounted and unhooked the spade they had brought with them. 'I've only got one good hand, thanks to you,' he said. 'How d'ya expect me to dig? You'll have to do it yerself.'

Slim said nothing. He slid a knife from its sheath and cut Billy's hands free. 'Go help yer pa,' he said gruffly. 'Just remember, both of ya, that this pistol ain't fer decoration.'

Billy slid from his horse and took the spade from his pa. As they bent to the task Billy whispered, 'Is the money really here, Pa?'

Tom hesitated, then decided that Billy should know the truth. 'No, Billy, it ain't.'

'What we diggin' fer, then?'

'Time, son, an' some luck.'

'If ya wanna talk do it so I can hear,' Slim said. 'Otherwise shuddup.'

Tom wiped the sweat from his forehead and looked up. 'Possible someone got here afore us.'

'Hope not, fer your sake,' Slim said. 'Patience is running out.'

Tom winked at Billy as the earth piled up around

them. 'Think we've struck something,' he called. Then, quietly so that Slim would not hear, he whispered, 'If ya get the chance run fer it an' hide. Then stay down. Don't worry 'bout me. I'll take care of myself and find you later.'

As he had hoped, Slim slid from the saddle and came closer to see what they had found. Was it close enough? Tom knew this may be his only chance. He also knew the odds were stacked heavily against him. Slim was alert and dangerous. He gripped the spade in his left hand and tensed his muscles.

'There he is!' The shout came unexpectedly from down the street where two men were advancing upon them. 'That's one o' the varmints!' Shots sounded.

If luck was what Tom was digging for, he had found it, for Slim's attention was momentarily distracted. Tom had only a split second to take advantage of the chance that fate had thrown at him. He swung the spade and, although Slim saw it coming, it caught him hard on one kneecap. The blow might not have fractured the bone but it was sufficient to incapacitate the bounty hunter long enough for Tom to leap at him and wrest his pistol from his hand.

He stared at the men who had yelled and recognized them as those he had humiliated on the trail from the ranch. Their intention was plain.

'Run!' He turned to urge his son away but the boy had already gone. 'Well done,' he muttered as he raced for the cover of the nearest alley.

As he glanced back he saw from the corner of his eye that Slim had reached his horse and was withdrawing the rifle from its scabbard. What happened to him after that Tom didn't know but more shots cracked, some of which came from the Winchester. They were too close for comfort, one clipping his upper thigh and sending intense pain down his leg.

Then he reached the alley, threw himself into it to be protected by the walls of the buildings on either side. He knew that wouldn't last. He could hear the pounding of feet coming closer. Of course, the men had seen where he'd gone. He moved further in. Everything about these men spoke of professional gunmen. They were after vengeance and he was the target.

The odds were definitely not in his favour this time. He was now alone fighting two hard men, possibly three. He was handicapped by having his right hand unable to wield a gun; by the wound in his leg which prevented him from moving fast; by worry about whether his son was safe and by concern that Slim, if he had managed to seek safety, would also be on his tail.

There was only one thing in his favour: the fading light. Soon the flickering oil lamps from windows would be the only source of illumination in the back alleys where the dim light of the moon could not penetrate. At least he was armed but could not afford to waste bullets by taking useless shots.

He couldn't expect help. This was his fight. In fact, on hearing the shots, the citizens were more likely to take cover inside their own homes or in the stores – wherever security could be found.

He stopped, crouched low in the shadows, and listened. The sounds of pursuit had receded but he knew the men would not have given up. Once sighting their quarry, men such as these kept on until someone died, for there was death in their Colts and they knew how to dispense it.

Tom continued to limp down the alley into the back lots, taking shelter by a low wall. He realized he wasn't safe where he was but there weren't many other places to hide.

'We know where you are an' we're comin' to get ya.' The taunting voice came to him from the shadows further down to his right. That was worth knowing, but too close for comfort. And where was the second man?

He held his breath, straining for the slightest sound, but heard nothing. He shifted position. Did they really know where he was?

Then his question was answered as a gun cracked and a slug struck the wall a mere six inches from his head. Perhaps they hadn't seen him and that was just a lucky shot. But he couldn't risk it.

He moved cautiously to his left. A second shot smacked into a wooden post, sending splinters into his face.

'Goddammit!' he muttered. It was possible he was being driven into the path of the second man so he changed course, sliding along the wall, searching for a door or an opening. Still, he held his fire.

'Wanna give up?' the taunting voice called again.

'Yer've gotta find me first.' Immediately he had replied he rolled across the alley to the other side, gritting his teeth against the pain in his injured limbs.

This time the gunmen's response came from both

directions, the flashes of their Colts giving away their positions, the bullets hitting the spot where he had been only seconds before.

'We're gonna get ya, you sonofabitch.' There was a sense of excitement at the thrill of the chase.

Tom felt no such elation; anger rather than fear that these men considered themselves somehow invulnerable. He had no pleasure in hiding but it was two against one, he was wounded and he had only six bullets in his gun. He had to even the odds. How to do that, though, was far from obvious.

He had to stay alive, find Billy, get Dave out of jail and settle things with Slim. To stay where he was gave the advantage to his pursuers so he continued his search for somewhere to get out of the alley where he felt the men were closing in on him.

He had to take the fight to them but first he had to find a way to evade them and to bind his injury. He could feel the warmth of blood drifting down to his boots.

He stood up and moved as fast as he could. It was impossible not to make a noise but that was of less importance than surprising the gunmen. Shots followed his movements as he felt the hardness of the low wall under his searching hand. Without pausing he climbed over it and, in the gloom, made out a single-storey building ahead.

No shots followed but the footsteps behind informed him that he was not going to get away so easily.

He reached the building, which appeared to be a store with a heavy wooden door which, as he pulled at it, opened easily. There seemed to be no windows. Could he conceal himself here? He went in and pulled the door shut, steadied his breathing and waited. The inside was in total darkness. Had he walked into a trap of his own making?

He felt his way to the wall and sat down with his back against it. His leg was paining him badly and he needed to stem the loss of blood, although in the dark he couldn't tell how bad it was. The wound in his arm was also bleeding again.

By feel alone he removed his bandanna and bound it over the torn flesh of his leg. It was the best he could do.

From the brief glimpse of the building he had taken as he stepped inside he guessed he was in some kind of store about ten feet by twenty with racks and packages piled up against the walls. Machinery or tools, he guessed. There were no windows and as far as he could tell no other way in or out.

A catch on the inside of the door had secured it but he reckoned that would not last long against a determined attack. But, did the men know he was there? He'd no idea how close they were when he had found refuge.

The marshal, having surprised Alice and her pa with the information he had given them, sat up quickly as the sound of gunfire resounded further down the street.

He took a long draw of his third cigarette, ground it out on the floor and levered himself to his feet. 'Sounds

141

like some polecat's shootin' up my town,' he said. 'I gotta go see to it. You two stay put. No sense in getting yerselves shot.'

They watched him go, and sat in silence as they digested what they had been told.

'Seems Tom's a good man,' Dave said at last. 'He didn't kill my son. He can't be blamed for what his uncle did.'

'I judged him wrong,' Alice agreed. 'D'you think Billy knows he's not Tom's son?'

'Dunno nothin' about that. What I do know is that Tom saved my life, probably yours and yer ma's as well, and he wouldn't have left me in jail without some plan to get me out. I also know he has an eye for you,' he added with a grin. He stood. 'I'm goin' outside whether the marshal wants me to or not. I've gotta know what's going on.'

He retrieved his Colt, checked it and slid it into its holster.

'I'm coming with you,' Alice said and held up her hand to forestall her pa's objection.

By the time they entered the street the sound of gunfire was fainter, coming from the rear of the buildings. With the danger being less imminent, many more folk had come out to see what was going on.

'Could be Tom's ruse to get the marshal away from the office,' Dave suggested doubtfully. 'Mebbe we'll see him in a moment as he comes to break me out.'

In the absence of any immediate danger they strolled along the boardwalk a short way. 'Don't reckon we should go too far,' Dave said.

Alice was about to agree when she suddenly cried out. 'There's Billy!' The boy was running hard in their direction, peering fearfully over his shoulder.

'Billy!' Alice called. 'Over here!'

He rushed over to them. Breathlessly he blurted out, 'Pa's bein' chased by two shooters. A man called Slim tied me up and then made us come into town to dig up some money. Then Pa hit him with a spade an' two men came shootin' at us an' Pa told me to run. An then—'

'Stop!' Dave told him, placing a calming hand on the boy's shoulder. 'Let's go back to the marshal's office an' you can tell us all about it.'

'But Pa needs help.'

'We'll help him, of course, but first you gotta calm down an' let us make sense of what you're saying.' Dave gently propelled him into the law office. 'Now, where is ya pa an' this man ya call Slim?'

'Dunno where Slim is. But Pa had to run fer it, over the back. I saw the two men go after him. I think he's bin hurt.'

'OK, Billy. You stay here with Alice an' I'll go see what I kin do to help yer pa.'

'Be careful, Pa,' Alice said.

'Goes without saying.'

'Who'd want to kill Tom?'

'Tell you later.' He did not need to ask who the shooters were. He had a very good idea.

CHAPTER 14

'We got the goddamn coyote!' A voice filled with triumph reached Tom through the thick wood of the door. 'We know ya in there. If ya come out now we promise to give ya the chance to make a run fer it.' Subdued laughter followed this.

But run for it? He found it difficult to move fast. He listened and heard them talking together but could only make out some of the words. It seemed they were discussing whether to force the door, burn him out or just wait. He reckoned waiting was the very last option they'd choose.

Then he heard Seth say, 'I'm goin' round to the back jus' to make sure he cain't git out that way.' His footsteps receded. Was this a trick to entice him out? He didn't know but he had to take a chance. He had to do something, not just wait around to be shot.

He checked his gun as well as he could in the dark, then dropped to his belly on the hard floor. By keeping his head as low as possible he could peer out through the gap between the door and the ground with one eye.

From that position he was relieved to see, against the faint light from outside, the movement of Cato's feet as he paced up and down.

'Cato,' he called. 'If I come out what sorta chance will ya give me?'

Cato gave a short laugh and his feet came nearer to the door. 'More'n ya'll git if ya stay where ya are.'

He noticed that Cato's feet had stopped moving. Keep him talking. 'Have I got yer word on that?'

'Yeah, but make it quick. I'm sorta gettin' tired.'

Tom felt the door give a little as Cato pushed against it. He could hardly have asked for better. He held his Colt with the barrel pointing through the gap under the door. Although the gun was too thick to go into the gap he hoped there was sufficient room for the passage of a bullet. He aimed as well as he could and pulled the trigger four times.

Each slug, travelling no more than six inches, hit its target. Each smashed into Cato's feet or ankles. A scream of agony brought a smile to Tom's face. He scrambled to his feet even before the sound of the shots had died. It was now or never.

He released the door catch and thrust hard. The door swung open and struck Cato fully on the shoulder, sending him staggering back before his legs gave way and he fell to the ground, writhing in agony. At least one of his feet was a mass of blood, leather and bone.

Nevertheless, with eyes smouldering with hatred and pain, he managed to raise his pistol and swing it in Tom's direction.

'Don't!' Tom said. But Cato wasn't listening. Tom

couldn't wait. He fired once, the slug taking Cato full in the chest, his gun flying from his lifeless hand.

Running footsteps warned him that Seth was coming fast. As he forced himself to move he stooped to pick up Cato's gun. He grabbed for it, then realized too late his mistake as the blood on his hand caused the gun to slip from his grasp. As Seth's shadowy form appeared around the corner, he made his escape, leaving Cato's pistol behind.

Tom threw himself into the darkness of the alleyway opposite. Seth followed with several shots but Tom crouched low, keeping close to the wall.

'I'm comin' fer ya, ya sonofabitch,' Seth roared. He was not to know how little ammunition Tom had.

Tom kept moving. The acrid smell of cordite quickened his senses. He looked for somewhere to hide. He saw ahead the outline of a two-storey building, one of the stores fronting onto the main street. Wooden steps led up to a door. He began to climb, hauling on the rail to take the strain.

Two shots sounded and a bullet singed his hair and buried itself in the balustrade. Another plucked at his jacket. He realized he had made a second mistake; up here he was exposed.

He tried the door but it was firmly locked. He fired a shot into the lock and the door flew inwards. He fell through the opening as more slugs smacked into the woodwork.

He lay flat, looking back along the alleyway, searching for movement but seeing nothing but shadows. He examined his surroundings and found he was in a storeroom with boxes piled against walls and filling shelves. Stairs at the far end of the room led down to street level.

Realizing that he couldn't stay where he was, he crossed the room and took the stairs down into a mercantile store. There were two windows flanking the entrance door, which, as he should have expected, was also locked.

Footsteps sounded above his head and he knew he had to act fast. As a shot rang out he picked up a heavy stool and smashed it against the larger of the two windows, then hurled himself through the broken pane. Just before he hit the boardwalk in a shower of glass he rolled into a ball, tumbled down the three steps and landed in the dust of the main street.

The pain almost made him lose consciousness but through all of this he had managed to hold on to his Colt and, in what was a reflex action, he span round and fired at the gunman who had followed him through the window.

There was only a click as the hammer fell on the empty chamber. 'Dammit,' he muttered and looked up into the eyes of the man who was going to kill him.

But Seth wasn't ready to deliver the fatal shot. Not without gloating. 'You sonofabitch,' he grated, clearly enjoying the situation. 'Yer've bin sticking ya horn in where it's not wanted. Now I'm gonna kill ya slow. Say yer prayers.'

His finger tightened on the trigger as a cry came from across the street. 'Hold it right there!'

Seth, professional gunman that he was, swung around, dropped to a crouch to face this new threat and fired when he saw his target. Tom groaned as he saw Dave fall back and lay unmoving on the boardwalk. He climbed to his feet and lunged but the distance was too great. He was still five feet away when Seth swung back.

'Not so fast,' Seth snarled. That was the last sound he made. From further along the street a rifle spoke and Seth took lead through his heart.

Tom looked up. Buck Clements was striding along the centre of the street with his Winchester cradled in his arm. 'Seems like I was just in time,' he said as he drew nearer.

'I'm more'n obliged,' Tom said. He pointed to Dave's inert form. 'I owe ya both.'

The marshal helped him across the street and, discovering that Dave was still conscious, they lifted him into a sitting position and examined his wound.

'He needs the doc,' the marshal said, then noticed the blood on Tom's clothes. 'And so do you.'

'What the hell did ya think you were doing?' Tom asked Dave, becoming aware for the first time of the blood running down his own face where the glass had sliced his flesh.

'He'd've killed ya,' Dave whispered.

'Yeah. So he would,' Tom grinned. 'The marshal here was a mite slow. I'm indebted to ya.'

'No you're not!' Dave murmured.

'We need some help,' Buck Clements said. He called some men over. Together they picked Dave up and carried him down the street to the doc's surgery.

'Where's Billy and Alice?' Tom asked the marshal

while the doc's wife was dressing his own wounds.

'Safe in the law office,' Dave said. 'I told them to stay there.'

Buck Clements said, 'I'll go tell 'em the good news.'

'No you won't,' Tom growled. 'I wanna see my son. It's bin a helluva long day but there's one more thing I have to do before it's over.'

The doc's wife placed a restraining hand on his shoulder as he tried to rise from the chair where she was treating him. 'Nearly finished.'

Billy had been ashamed of himself for running away when his pa was in danger. He had been a coward, although he didn't know what he could have done otherwise.

But now, knowing that his pa was being chased by two gunmen, he had scuttled into the lawman's office and was sheltering behind the skirts of a woman.

'I wanna go out an' help,' he told Alice.

'You can't do that,' Alice said. 'We both have to stay here. The marshal and my pa are out there somewhere and they've both got guns. We're better off where we are. We'd only get in the way.'

Billy sat in the marshal's chair and idly pulled open the drawers of the desk. In one he saw a .45 partially covered with papers. He pulled it out and examined it. The chambers were empty but he weighed it in his hands. He could find no bullets.

'I know how to use this,' he said.

'I expect you do but you're not going to.'

Billy dropped the gun in his lap. 'I'd like to be a

marshal when I get old enough.'

'It's a dangerous profession,' Alice suggested.

'I'm not afraid.' Billy puffed out his chest then let all the air out of his lungs. The truth was that today he had been scared and he wasn't proud of that.

Alice was about to say something when the office door opened. They looked up sharply, expecting to see one or all of the men. Instead Billy let out a gasp as he recognized Slim. Alice glanced at him questioningly.

'It's him,' Billy said.

Alice quickly realized who Slim was as he slammed the door shut, leaned heavily against it and said, 'My luck's in. Two birds fer the price of one!' His gaze swept appreciatively over Alice's trim figure. 'You're the gal in the saloon.'

'She's nobody,' Billy said quickly. 'Jus' come in to see the marshal. But he ain't here. She's nothing to do with anything. She was jus' going.'

Slim kept his eyes on Alice. 'Interesting. But she ain't going nowhere. Not just yet, anyway.' He walked across the room and stood by the stove where a pot of coffee was being heated. 'We'll all make oursel's comfortable. Fact is, the lady can get us all some coffee while we're waiting.'

'I told ya, she ain't nothin' to do—'

Slim's voice remained quiet but he might as well have shouted. 'I know what ya told me. But since ya so all-fired to be so helpful you kin pour out the coffee instead. Now git to it!'

'It's OK, Billy,' Alice said. 'Best do like he says.'

As he rose from the creaky chair Billy carefully placed the Colt on the seat out of sight. He went over to the stove, set out three mugs, took up a cloth and used it to pick up the pot. Making a pretence of pouring the coffee he swung the pot hard, aiming the contents at Slim's face.

But the man saw it coming, moving quickly, and the hot liquid splashed against the wall and ran harmlessly down in little rills.

Slim stepped in and his clenched fist caught Billy hard on the side of the head, sending the boy across the floor to end up on his back, dazed and gritting his teeth against the pain.

Slim looked down at him, a half-smile on his face. 'If yer've got any more little tricks like that up yer sleeve best to keep 'em fer another day. That is,' he added, 'if ya live that long.'

Alice had rushed over to help Billy to his feet and back to the marshal's chair. With the edge of her skirt she dabbed at the blood oozing from his nose, then turned angrily to Slim. 'You're very brave, hitting a boy half your size. Why don't you leave right now before someone your own age gets here.'

Slim ignored the insult. 'Well, we'll have to do without the coffee,' he said. His hand dropped to the Colt in the holster at his hip as he saw Billy's surprised expression. 'Yeah, someone was kind enough to give me his gun after ya pa took mine. An' I'll use it if ya don't behave. Now shut up, the both of you.'

Billy knew he should just sit quiet but he couldn't. The gun he'd found in the desk drawer was in his hands again. It wasn't loaded but Slim was not to know that. He lifted it quickly and pointed it at the man's chest.

Attempting to make the command deep and firm he said, 'Take out yer gun, mister, an' drop it on the floor.'

Slim didn't move. 'You're a real tough young man, ain't ya? But, ya know, you're beginning to annoy me. Look, son, I don't wanna kill ya. You've still got plenty of livin' to do. All I want is yer pa's money, then we kin all go our own way. Including the young lady here. Less she'd prefer to come with me.'

Billy tried to hold the gun steady. 'I meant what I said.'

Slim shrugged. 'Before you kin pull that trigger, son, I kin have my pistol out an' fired twice. So don't be foolish.'

Billy hardly saw the movement. Perhaps he'd blinked. But a gun appeared in Slim's hand and was held steady, pointing straight at him. He lowered his own weapon, laying it carefully on the desk. He looked at Alice apologetically. 'Sorry,' he muttered.

'It's him should be sorry,' Alice said. 'What possible threat could we be?'

'He was aimin' to kill me,' Slim pointed out. 'Now, Billy, real careful, empty the slugs out so's you won't be tempted agin.'

'It's empty,' Billy said and spun the chamber to show him.

Slim guffawed as he replaced his Colt in its holster. 'Well, you sure got guts, kid, but that ain't gonna do ya no good if yer pa don't play the game my way.'

'I'm not a kid,' Billy said.

'Put the toy away, then.'

Billy laid the gun on his lap. 'I would've shot you,' he said.

'I'm sure you'd've tried.'

'And if Billy didn't I would've done,' Alice said.

Slim thought this droll. 'How cosy. But we can't stay here all day. I'm sure ya both know what I want. So,' he turned his gaze on Alice, 'you are gonna go to the doc's and find out from Billy's pa exactly where the money is.

'You're gonna tell him if you ain't back here with the answer he's gonna lose his son. Same goes if he tries the same sort of trick he tried earlier. I ain't a patient man. That clear?'

'What if he's not there?'

'He will be. I saw the three of them walking down after the two of 'em were shot. Ten minutes. After that things'll begin to happen.'

Billy drew in his breath.

Alice nodded. 'You won't get away with this.' She glanced at the boy. 'Your pa can't be too badly hurt, Billy. I'll let you know.' She turned on her heel and left.

After nearly ten minutes steps sounded on the board-walk outside. Slim, drawing his Colt, glared at Billy, signalling him to be silent.

Tom's voice sounded through the door. 'I'm comin' in. I ain't wearing.'

'Don't, Pa!' Billy yelled. 'He means to kill us both.' He didn't know whether that was true but he was scared.

Before he could say any more the door was pushed open and Tom entered, taking in the scene at a glance. His right arm, bandaged from elbow to wrist, was held against his chest by a neat sling as he limped over to the desk by his son. His gun-belt and gun were missing from his hip.

Billy remained seated in the chair and, in answer to the unspoken question, said, 'I'm OK, Pa.'

Slim, with his Colt pointed at Tom's chest, said with a note of triumph, 'Ah, the man himself! Sorry 'bout yer arm but I'd prefer to see it without the sling. Take it off, easy now. Don't know what you're hidin' in there.'

Tom slipped his arm out of the sling and let it hang by his side, easing it down with his other hand.

Slim relaxed and re-holstered his gun. 'I've stayed alive this long by being careful,' he grinned. 'Now's the time fer you to talk if ya want ya son to go on living.'

'And then you'll let us both go?'

'You have my word as a gentleman,' Slim smirked. When Tom didn't reply at once he slapped his holster, the meaning very clear. 'On the count of five, Deegan, I'm gonna draw.'

Tom's eyes held those of the bounty hunter. 'Why don't you and me settle this outside? Cowards shelter behind women and children.'

Slim's smile only exaggerated the cruelty behind it. 'Tempting,' he said. 'But I've had worse insults than that.'

'No!' Billy cried. He thought nobody could be as fast on the draw as this frightening man. 'He'd kill ya.'

'Might do that anyway,' Slim said. 'But think I'll pass up on ya offer this time.'

Billy, his nerves tingling, couldn't interpret the glance his pa shot in his direction. He was sure his pa was trying to send him a message. But what? He had tried twice to overpower the gunman, once with hot coffee and once with an empty gun, and had failed both times. Was he supposed to try again?

Then it struck him. He wasn't expected to take Slim on, rather to give his pa the chance to do so. He eyed the empty pistol. With a sudden movement of his arm he sent it scudding across the desk onto the floor until it hit the pot-bellied stove with a loud clang.

For a fleeting second Slim's attention was diverted. Only for a fleeting second, but in that short time a throwing knife had appeared in Tom's right hand from where it had been concealed in the bandages. In one fluent motion the slender steel blade flashed across the room into the gunman's neck. Blood gushed immediately as Slim sank to his knees, then fell onto his back.

Slim had managed to draw his Colt, a reflex action of his finger pulling the trigger as his other hand shot up in an attempt to pull the knife from his throat. They were the last conscious movements he ever made.

Billy watched open-mouthed as Tom strode across to the dead body and retrieved his blade.

'Sorry ya had to witness that, Billy,' his pa said, sinking wearily into a chair and letting his breath out in a long sigh. 'But ya did well. If ya'd go get the marshal I reckon we kin go home.'

EPILOGUE

It was three months later, on a hot and windless afternoon, that the wedding of Tom Deegan and Alice Green took place in the church of Salvation. The ladies of the town made it an excuse to wear their prettiest dresses; the men put on their best clothes; the children were given a holiday from school.

The only thing missing was the sonorous voice of the preacher, Morgan Jones, as he urged the folk of Salvation to abide by the teachings of the good Lord.

The general opinion was that Alice looked radiant in a blue skirt and blouse and was the envy of many girls who had yet to find themselves a husband, for Tom looked particularly handsome that day.

The church itself was bathed in light, the bell tower catching the sun. Billy was happy with the outcome of his pa's brief courtship.

'Is it all right with you, Billy, if I ask Alice to marry me?' Tom had asked and Billy had nodded. Yes, he liked Alice.

Her ma and pa had also been happy. They had seen

it coming.

At the end of the ceremony, as the happy couple stood outside the church with their guests, Tom whispered to his new wife and went across to speak to the marshal.

He spoke softly. 'I've kept my secret too long,' he said. 'Now I've bin lucky enough to win me a beautiful wife there's somethin' I've gotta clear up. Thirteen years I've kept silent. I had a good life with my son an' didn't reckon on spoilin' that. Time I made a clean start, get things off my conscience.'

'Why'd ya wanna tell me?' Buck Clements asked. 'If yer got a confession to make there's better places to make it.'

Tom laid a hand on his shoulder. 'I'm doin' it cos you're a good man an' I kin trust you to do right. You want the best fer this town an' so do I. The town's got its law back an' John Gordon's had his wings clipped with the loss of six of his best gunslingers.'

'Dunno whether I've earned yer trust,' the marshal said. 'An' the Triple O is outside my bailiwick, but I'll have a talk with Bob Candy, the county sheriff over at Warnerville. He owes me a favour. 'Tween us we'll make sure John Gordon buys any land legal.'

Tom nodded. 'I know ya will. That's why I want to tell ya where the money's stashed from the hold-up, where I hid it all those years back.'

'Ya mean ya never touched any of it?'

'Weren't mine to use.'

'D'ya know how much it was?'

'Nope. I never looked. I haven't hankered to know

157

since an' I don't wanna know now.'

'It's bin hid fer years,' Buck Clements said. 'Rats might've eaten it.'

'A lotta folk've died on account of it. I don't wanna see no more killing. If it's still there you'll know what to do with it.'

'It'll have to be returned to where it rightly belongs.'

'Yeah. Will ya do that fer me?'

The marshal inclined his head. 'It's the right thing to do. Providin' it's still where ya stashed it.'

'Thanks. I left it in the saddle-bags wrapped in a tarp to keep it dry.' Tom moved closer.

Buck Clements waited patiently.

'After I'd spoken to my aunt about Billy I came into town looking fer somewhere safe. There would've bin more'n a day's ride to git there an' back if I was to put it where I was s'posed to. It was gettin' dark and I was desperate to get back home. I was terrified I'd be caught. I was hurtin' from the burns and I couldn't get the sight of the dead bodies outa my head.

'I'd nothing to bury the money with an' I had to get rid of it. As I passed the church, the one my uncle built, I had a great idea.' He spoke softly in the marshal's ear. 'Don't look up when I tell ya.'

'Why the hell should I. . . ?'

'I made my way up to the bell tower without being seen an' stuffed the bags in a corner. Nobody ever goes up there. I thought it fitting as my uncle's legacy seeing as how he had the church built.'

'I alus reckoned you knew where it was stashed,' the marshal said. He had the good sense not to raise his head but his eyes lifted upwards. 'It's a hell of a responsibility, but I'll do the best I can. I guess the reward offered still stands for conviction and return of the money.'

'If so, it'll be comin' your way. I don't want nothin' to do with it.'

'Well, whadyer want me to do with it?'

Tom considered that. 'Mebbe the orphanage could make use of it. I'd like to think the kids there might get the chance my uncle gave me.'

'Ya trust me to do all that?'

Tom smiled. 'Yeah, I trust ya.'

'There's somethin' I don't understand,' the marshal said. 'Why'd ya keep quiet about the money all this time?'

Tom thought for a long moment. 'Don't rightly know, 'cept I was only sixteen at the time. I couldn't trust no one, not Marshal Brady, not you, nor anyone else I could've told.

'Then later, as time passed and I had a son to look after, I didn't reckon I should risk being put on trial as part of the gang. Seemed easier to forget about it an' I tried to do just that.'

'Why tell me now?'

'Alice's idea. Said she wouldn't marry me if I didn't.'

'A man can't fight agin those odds,' Buck Clements said.

'Wouldn't even try.' Tom went across to his wife and put his arm around her.